'Within a few pages I was hooked by a marvellous novel.'
Daily Telegraph

'A hotel which celebrates Christmas all year round provides a
hilarious background for a novel about how families work—or not.'
Guardian

'Geraldine McCaughrean is so inventive . . . a thrilling read.'
Melvin Burgess, *Books for Keeps*

'A richly comic drama of character and response to the unexpected whose surreal out-of-time setting enables a unique take on the meaning of Christmas, ritual, illusion and reality.'

Elizabeth Hammill, *Books For Keeps*

'A wonderfully inventive story, with intriguing characters and superbly realised plot . . . McCaughrean is a superb writer who builds stories which flicker in the mind long after the book has been laid aside, and who leaves puzzles to solve and issues to consider. A treasure and a pleasure for readers between ten and a hundred and ten.'

Carousel

FOREVER
X

Other books by Geraldine McCaughrean

GERALDINE McCAUGHREAN

FOREVER

X

OXFORD
UNIVERSITY PRESS

OXFORD

UNIVERSITY PRESS

Great Clarendon Street, Oxford OX2 6DP

Oxford University Press is a department of the University of Oxford.
It furthers the University's objective of excellence in research, scholarship,
and education by publishing worldwide in

Oxford New York

Auckland Cape Town Dar es Salaam Hong Kong Karachi
Kuala Lumpur Madrid Melbourne Mexico City Nairobi
New Delhi Shanghai Taipei Toronto

With offices in

Argentina Austria Brazil Chile Czech Republic France Greece
Guatemala Hungary Italy Japan Poland Portugal Singapore
South Korea Switzerland Thailand Turkey Ukraine Vietnam

Oxford is a registered trade mark of Oxford University Press
in the UK and in certain other countries

British Library Cataloguing in Publication Data available

ISBN: 978-0-19-275496-7

1 3 5 7 9 10 8 6 4 2

Printed in Great Britain by CPI Cox & Wyman, Reading, RG1 8EX

Paper used in the production of this book is a natural,
recyclable product made from wood grown in sustainable forests.
The manufacturing process conforms to the environmental
regulations of the country of origin.

For Gill and Tim

1
Snow

There was a thud, and Joy woke to the impression that it was snowing. A blizzard of white flurried past the car window. This was odd, given the sweat crawling down inside her T-shirt. It recalled to mind illness, feverishness, hallucinations.

'Damn,' said her father.

'What happened?'

'Fancy a seagull, this far from the sea,' said her mother.

It was August and ninety degrees in the shade. Mr Shepherd had hit a seagull and holed the radiator. Shortly afterwards, the car began to overheat, so that steam drifted past the windows like dense winter fog.

All along the motorway they had been passing broken-down cars and vans and motorcaravans, their passengers spilled out on to the hard shoulder. Mr Shepherd had small hopes of getting a breakdown vehicle without a wait of several hours, and Mrs Shepherd had heard that the hard shoulder of a motorway was the single most dangerous place in the entire universe. So they struck off cross-country at the next exit, looking for a garage, and found themselves among the tarns and fells of the Lake District.

'We might just not get to Linstock tonight,' warned Dad. 'We may have to stay over somewhere here.'

No one in the car said anything. No one dared to speak the treachery of what they were thinking. Each summer the Shepherd family spent their annual holiday in Linstock, in a caravan in the back garden of Gran and Grandpa Shepherd's semi. Joy was of the opinion they could all just as easily stay home and shut themselves in the fridge, and save on petrol. But she only thought it. To say so out loud would have been disloyal. Even though everyone was thinking the same. Every summer without fail they spent two weeks in that caravan. Only twenty miles from the sea, it was, and right under the motorway.

Perhaps the car picked up on all their unspoken yearnings *not* to reach Linstock and that caravan. For all of a sudden it stopped. There was no garage within sight, no telephone, no roadside houses, nothing—only a long purple valley and a lake scrawled on, like pale blue paper, by whole sentences of ducks, punctuated with moorhens and exclamations of sunlight.

Jack Shepherd rolled the car into a farm gateway, safely off the road, and everyone stood around it, helpless, marooned. Only Mel went on sleeping, sprawled across his mother's shoulder. Little children could sleep through the End of the World.

There was no gate to the farm track, only a cattle grid, and beside it—like a blessed sign from God in the wilderness—a wooden door-panel painted with the words '*B & B/Full Board*' and a snowflake.

'That's it, then,' said Mr Shepherd nodding at the sign. 'Don't let's leave anything in the car.'

He never left anything in the car, assuming that car thieves dogged his tracks with gleaming eyes and wolfish resolve to strip the Fiesta bare. So he heaved all the suitcases out now and, with his wife carrying Mel, led his family off along the track towards the promise of bed-and-breakfast.

Broad and dusty, the cart-track climbed the fellside steadily, coiling round the hill, round and up, the view gradually growing into larger and larger vistas of deep grass, tumbling scree, sky-filled lake, sunbleached rocks. They passed an electrical substation humming like the distant, unseen motorway, way, way off. The air was dense, breeze-less, and had to be waded through, as though in the heat it had thickened like gravy. Flies and midges circled over rabbit and sheep droppings, the only movement in a landscape too hot to move.

'I'm thirsty,' said Joy. 'Will they have something to drink? What if they're full? What if they're away on holiday?' Questions rose like larks out of the ground, but it was too hot for anyone to bother answering them.

Suddenly Mr Shepherd shouted, 'Mind yourselves!' and a slab of metal and glass hurtled down on them trailing dust: a 42-seater coach, empty but for its driver.

Seeing pedestrians on the path, the driver slowed the coach to a crunching skid, nodded his red-cheeked head at them. 'All right?' he called brightly.

Mr Shepherd opened his mouth to answer, but the coach driver, stirring his way through the gears, put his foot down and sped away like a glossy mirage.

'I bet he scrapes the car,' said father looking disconsolately back down the track.

Even so, in a landscape worryingly untouched by the twentieth century, the coach was a hopeful sign. The Shepherds righted their wheel-along suitcases and hauled them round the next bend in the everlasting track.

And there it was—a large white building, its brown lawn marked out by miniature pine trees, a gravel car park as streaked with oil as an English beach, a black tin barn. Mel woke and was instantly delighted. 'A donkey!' he said.

Anne Shepherd looked her children over and tweaked at their damp, dark hair and her own, hoping to present a good impression. But in the light of the sweaty T-shirts, the dusty trainers, the chocolate stains, she instructed everyone to look as appealing as possible.

Abandoning the suitcases, they crowded into the square of

shade beneath the porch. 'You're duly warned,' said their mother crisply, 'I shall cry if we're turned away.' Jack Shepherd knocked.

As they waited, Joy let her eyes run idly over the house. The names of the proprietors were written across the lintel: *Licensed for the sale of . . . Props: Colin and Ivy Partridge*. There was an English Tourist Board car sticker in the glass of the front door, and each pane had white sediment in one corner. Despite the bright sunlight, at this close range, Joy could see now that a string of dirt-caked, dislodged light bulbs snaked to and fro beside the porch. By turning her head sideways she could just make out that the bulbs formed letters, words: FOREVER X. A further group of unlit bulbs had clumped together underneath, like purple grapes left to wither on the vine.

There was music playing indoors—loud laughter and a man's voice. The laughter gained momentum as it came towards them, and thudded heavily against the far side of the door. Their knocking must have gone unheard, for the man who opened up was not expecting to find anyone on the step. He was elderly, with wild white hair and a beard hooked on over his ears. Thanks to this stifling gag of nylon wool, the thick, red, high-necked jacket, red trousers, wellington boots, and scarlet mittens, his face was an apoplectic smudge of melting purple, his eyes bulging and wide. At the sight of strangers blocking his way, he reeled and gave an inarticulate grunt. Then, recovering himself, he bared at them a fine set of porcelain dentures, and began to nod and laugh and laugh and nod. 'Eeh, grand,' he said. 'Just grand!' A shaking hand reached out to chuck Mel under the chin, then the old man lunged through, scattering the Shepherds off the doormat, and made for the barn, head down saying, 'Merry Christmas! Merry Christmas, one and all, yes.' Mel stared after him, eyes wide, silenced by ecstasy and bewilderment.

'Have you booked?' Catching sight of the Shepherds as she hurried between dining room and kitchen, a woman came to the door, picking up a desk diary from the hall table as she came.

'We broke down,' said Mr Shepherd, off balance. 'The car.'

'Do you by any chance have a vacancy for tonight?' said his wife appealingly. 'Absolutely anything would do!'

'It's tea time,' said Ivy Partridge, shrilly accusing. And then, 'You'd best come in. I'll have to finish off the old ladies first.' As she opened the door to the dining room, not a muscle of her face flinched from a fusillade of gunshots. Joy deduced afterwards that the noise must have been crackers.

The Shepherds waited, mesmerized by the sight and ting-ting-tinging of angel chimes spinning above four lighted candles on the hall table. Somewhere under the stairs, Bing Crosby was singing, though to a different beat.

When Mrs Partridge returned, she thrust a plate of hot mince pies under their noses. 'It's all right,' she said with a fleeting smile, 'I've set the Queen's Speech going. That should keep them happy for ten minutes. I'll show you up.' And she led the way to a large family bedroom.

An octopus of paper-chains hung between the centre lampshade and the picture rails. Tinsel garlands sagged in swags from bedpost to bedpost, while pop-up paper Santas pinned to the wall thrust out concertina bellies which had faded to pink in the brilliant sunshine. Behind the door, above the Fire Notice, a letter-heading had been taped to the wall. It said: *FOREVER XMAS: Christmas comes but once a year . . . except with us!*

'You'll not be stopping, then?' said Mrs Partridge. 'Just the one night, is it?' The Shepherds stood stranded in the narrow channels between the archipelago of beds, staring around them at prints of flying reindeer. 'Welcome to Forever Xmas. Supper's seven o'clock sharp. Tonight's Monopoly, and the video is *Miracle on 42nd Street*. I wouldn't leave your suitcases in the yard if I were you; coach might run them over when he comes back from pub. Happy Christmas and God bless us every one.'

Dropping the room key on the glass-topped dressing table, she straightened a felt stocking hanging from a drawer-knob, then hurried back along the corridor.

'Er . . . Excuse me . . . I wonder . . . please?' called Mrs Shepherd nervously after her. 'Is this . . . er . . . I mean to say . . . Is the Christmas bit obligatory?'

The hinge on the fire-door wheezed like a man punched in the stomach. 'I don't do *vegetarian*, if that's what you mean,' retorted Mrs Partridge and hurried back downstairs before the Queen could finish addressing the nation.

2
Turkeys

What a bonus! What a treat! To walk up a lane and find Christmas at the end of it! Joy prepared to be elated. As she watched Mel run from snow-caked window to tinselled toilet cistern, bouncing off the furniture like a ball in a pinball machine, she prepared to be, like him, entranced. And yet the situation was more odd than wonderful.

She looked to her parents for a clue, a cue: was it really Christmas all year round here? Had they stumbled on some portal in the space/time continuum which would grant them a summertime bite of the Christmas pie? The smells were right: the whole hotel reeked of roasting turkey and boiling pudding. The colours were right—everything red and green, from the carpets to the crockery. And yet. Outside the sun blazed down on Cold Pike until it vibrated like a white-hot anvil about to crack. There was whining and tapping at the windows, but it was neither the winter wynd nor Marley's ghost: it was mosquito and bluebottle. It felt odd.

Her mother, Joy noticed, chose the bed in the corner and kept sitting on it, as if to keep this unforeseen Christmas from creeping up on her. She too was uneasy. Dad simply kept wondering how much the car would cost, and fingering the hotel's tariff card. Finally his wife took it out of his hand and whispered, 'Think of the caravan.' After that, he read the newspaper instead. Perhaps that was his way of shutting out the strangeness.

Once a week, a refrigerated van left Kendal with twenty

turkeys for delivery to Forever Xmas. Each day two or three or four were set to roast in the extra-large ovens of Mrs Partridge's kitchen. She bought cranberry sauce by the crate from the cash-and-carry in Keswick, along with crackers and pudding and Paxo. For 364 days of the year, Colin and Ivy Partridge staged Christmas for anyone who, for whatever reason, omitted to celebrate it on December 25th.

Twice a week, a coach also brought parties of pensioners, friendly societies, women's clubs, British Legionnaires from the unfestive cities of Newcastle, Manchester, or Liverpool on outings to the fells and tarns of Wasthwaite to sing carols, eat turkey, and giggle at the folly of what they were doing. The day trippers gave themselves up to an afternoon of unreality, and left after tea-and-fruitcake.

But for those who stayed longer—two, maybe three nights—the game was played in earnest. Fathers who worked overseas, nurses and policemen on duty over Christmas, relations visiting from Australia—anyone cheated of a traditional British Christmas with their children—could look to Forever Xmas to supply the full gamut of festivities, from a blazing log fire to a visit from Father Christmas. Mrs Partridge's father filled that particular role, come rain, come snow, come heatwaves.

For the Shepherds, straying in on this 'unique tourist facility', it was a bizarre culture shock—like breaking into an asylum for the Christmasly insane. Ivy and Colin Partridge appeared to be the glummest people in all Cumbria: she with her hair rolled up round her head like an inflatable dinghy, he shiny with Brylcreem and over-ironing.

But the mechanic at the local garage said he had to send away for a spare part for the car. And it might take twenty-four hours to come.

That evening, when they went down to supper, there were four other tables occupied. Cliff Richard drizzled quietly out of speakers in all four corners of the room, and two of the turkey carcasses stood as centre-pieces to a buffet, with thick brown soup to start. All the windows were open, to encourage a through-draught, but since the sky outside was still a bright summery blue, the plush curtains had been drawn across to shut out the view of incandescent Cold Pike and to let the Christmas tree lights twinkle in the gloom.

At one table a huge muscular man with close-cropped hair barked loudly at a boy and a girl, like a boisterous dog wanting to be played with. 'Well then? Open it, open it!' A succession of shiny carrier bags were heaved across the table. The children responded—like shark fed on offal—with a feeding frenzy of eagerness, then played with large, noisy flashing vehicles and weapons on the table top, swerving between the plates, blasting each other across the pickle jars. Now and then, their mother mentioned table manners, but was ignored.

A party of Japanese teenage girls, dressed in expensive clothes, photographed each other in front of the Christmas tree, in front of the unlit Yule log, in front of the turkey carcasses, and raising their glasses in a toast to Christmas. Though the food was repugnant to them, they were observing the true customs of a foreign country, and they did it with the scrupulous, methodical thoroughness their friends would expect of them when they arrived home with their incomprehensible memories and two thousand photographs.

At another table, a father harangued his two daughters furiously, banging with the handle of his knife on the table and scowling and whispering loudly, while the children sat round-shouldered, eyelids half-closed against the onslaught of criticism. Only occasional snatches of the tirade reached as far as Joy. 'Look at you . . . way she dresses you . . . that woman . . . if I had any say . . . wouldn't be allowed . . . ' His children ate in silence, their eyes drifting to the tree as at home they drifted to the refuge of a TV set.

Last of all, in the darkest corner of the room, a man and boy sat opposite each other, his hands spread over the boy's, their platefuls of food barely touched. They seemed to have nothing whatsoever to say to one another.

Joy's mother was feeling guilty. Her relief at *not* reaching Linstock and the caravan pricked like a goad. Guiltily, she kept going to the pay phone in the hall to call Gran and Grandpa and say how sorry she was they had been delayed. The line was busy. She tried every five minutes. She was also worried about the effect Forever Xmas was having on Mel.

'What do you mean? He's in heaven,' said Joy.

'Exactly,' said Mrs Shepherd watching the four year old croon to himself as he gazed at the Christmas tree. 'All these people having Christmas, and we're not.'

'Aren't we? How can you tell?' asked Joy. She had just then been trying to get to grips with the philosophy of the thing. Was it the date—25th December—which constituted Christmas, or was it what people did by consensus on 25th December which made 25th December Christmas? That is to say, was 25th December still Christmas on uninhabited islands, even with no one to observe it? Or could August 12th just as well be Christmas if, by public accord, the world agreed to have it then? Was it all in the anticipation, perhaps? The result of people expecting it to happen? Had they, the Shepherds, jumped out on it and taken Christmas by surprise wearing its curlers and without a smile on its face? Or did the weather have something to do with it . . . ?

At this point, Mel, suddenly remembering that socks were crucial to Christmas, pulled off his shoes and threw them across the table. Brown Windsor soup tipped, like slurry from a dredger, into Joy's lap, and a glass of orange juice went over too.

10

'You'd best go and get changed,' said her mother. 'Rinse it through before it stains.'

'I've finished anyway,' said Joy.

'You don't want this Christmas pud?' said her father reaching across.

'Children don't,' said Joy scornfully. Lately she had noticed how often her father needed telling such things. The knowledge did not seem to be inborn, as it was in mothers.

No, she thought, as she battled upstairs through a dozen spring-loaded fire-doors, the weather could have nothing to do with it. Australians always had this kind of weather at Christmas. So where was it, then, Christmas? Without knowing, Joy was in search of it now—behind the fire-doors, beyond earshot of 'Jingle Bells'. She opened the door of their bedroom . . .

. . . And found an elf crouching in the fire-grate with her hand up the chimney.

She was large for an elf, small for a teenager—a pinch-faced, dark-haired girl in white tights and a green sateen blouse rucked at the seams and creased at the elbows and shirt-tail. She wore a carrier bag over her hand so that the soot from the chimney did not dirty her sleeve. She wore ballet shoes and red face-painted cheeks which exaggerated the paleness of her skin and made her look feverish, embarrassed.

'What are you doing?' said Joy. 'I'm going to get my dad.'

'No! Wait! I was just . . . ' The elf jumped up. She was about Joy's age, eleven or twelve, and painfully thin, with darting dark eyes. 'I was just doing you for wishes.'

Joy barred the door, arms folded. She had ambitions to be in the police. The elf had ambitions to get away, that much was plain. 'Doing us for what?' said Joy.

'You know? The forms? Your Christmas wish? Haven't you filled yours in yet?'

'What forms?'

'You know? Everybody gets one. Letter to Santa. Fill in the gaps. What you want. From Santa. Mam likes to know. Supposed to leave them in the grate. I collect them. Sometimes people shove them up the chimney. That's where I was . . .' She managed to combine a look of sleepiness with a desperate agitation—like an insomniac craving a good night's sleep. Joy flopped on to one of the beds. The elf sat down on another with a gesture of defeat. 'You're not supposed to see me,' she said. 'I'm not supposed to talk to the visitors.'

But she did.

Holly was the only daughter of Colin and Ivy Partridge; also their only elf. The firm of Forever Xmas was a family enterprise and did not earn sufficient to employ outside staff. So Holly came home from school to a perpetual round of elf-help: waiting at table, cleaning rooms, wrapping gifts, and playing with little children. People did not often bring children of Holly's age to Forever Xmas. The sudden and unexpected sight of Joy seemed to breach some dam inside her and out poured trade secrets.

'The lottery's made things easier,' said the elf, crossing her laddered white legs. 'Now most people wish to win the lottery. So they get lottery dice. Cheap. They used to put "the Premium Bonds" or the pools. Too expensive. Gift vouchers are ten pounds a go. We couldn't do it. Now it's lottery dice. 99p all up. The turkeys on the coaches are easiest: the old folk. Children want *so much*; write down masses of things. No end to it. The old folk, they either want peace in the world or to win the lottery.'

'What do they get if they ask for peace?' asked Joy, drawn into this grotto world of wish-fulfilment.

'A Marks and Spencer's voucher. Quite often they wish to get back together soon with Bill or Eric—a husband or something—someone who's dead. People are funny about wishing if they think nobody might read it.'

'What then? Do you kill them off or give them a wreath?'

'No. We bung them a bottle of Sanatogen—in case being run down is making them weepy. *I* wanted to do them pirate videos of *Stairway to Heaven* with David Niven, but Mam said old people don't have VCRs much . . . We do *try*, you know.' She said it defensively, resentfully, as if Joy had impugned her professionalism as an elf. And yet every strand of her fine, dishevelled hair dripped disillusionment. 'It's worse when the kids . . . ' (she said it as if she were not one, had never been one) 'when the kids ask for things like that too. *Wish Mum and Dad would stop fighting*—things like that. That's a killer.' And suddenly, quite unexpectedly, big tears rolled down on to her red cheeks and skidded off in all directions across the greasy paint. Joy recoiled, her sandal buckle snagging the candlewick bedcover. For the first time that day, she wished she was in Linstock.

The elf blew her nose. 'They used to like Christmas—Mam and Dad. Their favourite time, it was. Some people say it just makes extra work and costs a lot. But Mam and Dad they loved it. Got married at Christmas. Had me . . . All those old films TV puts on at Christmas: Mam and Dad love all them. It came to them in a flash. Nowhere else does it. There had to be a place for it. "In business, all you need is a good idea," Dad said. Year-round Christmas. That was their good idea.'

'And now they hate it,' said Joy, meaning to be sympathetic.

Her voice startled the elf into an awareness that she had spoken out of turn. 'I didn't say that! Of course not! Mam'd kill me if I said that. I didn't say that. It's all right. It's fine.' With a look of guilty panic, Holly Partridge jumped up, straightened the rumpled bedcover and, picking up the waste-paper basket to empty, darted out of the room.

Back at the dinner table Mum and Dad had had a bottle of wine and were holding hands. Dad had had to put the business supplement of his *Telegraph* under the wet tablecloth to save the shine. Even though the shine was Formica. It left him nothing to do but talk to his wife. Mel was playing in the Adventure Corner—a plastic slide, a foam cushion, and three beanbags.

'I brought these down from the bedroom,' said Mum, suddenly and gleefully remembering. She brought the questionnaires out of her bag and held them at arm's length to read. *A LETTER TO SNATA* said the misprint on the back. 'Apparently we have to fill them in and leave them in the fire-grate for Father Christmas,' she read.

'Snata Claus is coming to town,' said Dad derisively.

Anne Shepherd was giggly after the wine and ignored him. She wrote that she hoped the car would take a week to mend.

Joy said, 'I'll think about it. I don't know what to put,' and she folded the sheet and pocketed it. 'But we're not doing Christmas. You said.' She resolved not to fill it in at all, not to be one of the stereotypes Holly Partridge had divided the human race into.

But when Mel came running over, Joy at once offered him a lap and to write down his wishes for him. She would never have dreamed of denting the Christmas magic for her little brother, of trying to extinguish the shine in Mel's eyes.

'I want a white Power Ranger and a Megazord and a Mr Muscle and a Car Breakers . . . ' The shine turned to a gleam, a beady voracious hunger that made Mel curl and uncurl the fingers of both hands like a raptor stretching its claws.

Joy tried to quieten him—thought of the elf and wanted to silence and sooth him. 'Wouldn't you like to ask for something kind? What about all the little children who haven't got any toys or even enough to . . . Wouldn't you like to make a kind wish for th—'

She withered under Mel's glare. His top lip rucked into a snarl. 'No!' he said. 'I want a white Power Ranger and a Megazord and Mr Muscle . . . '

'Santa can't carry all that in this weather,' said Joy opening her knees so that her little brother slipped to the floor. 'He'd get heatstroke.'

'That's right,' said their mother gratefully. 'Things like that have to wait until December. What are you going to wish for, darling?' Tenderly she relinquished her husband's writing hand and found him a pen.

'A win on the lottery would do me nicely,' said Mr Shepherd, grinning round at them,

'*No!*' His daughter's ferocity startled him. '*No!*'

It startled Joy, too, to find she objected so much to her father's wish. But she did. She realized, with a pang of shame, that she was glaring at him, her mouth rucked into a snarl.

Mel began to grizzle and whine. Jack Shepherd screwed up his letter to Snata and pitched it into the open, unlit hearth saying, 'I tell you what: I wish this place were a thing of the past for all of us.' He pushed his face belligerently across the table at his disapproving children; wine always made him ratty in the end. 'I wish a plague on Father Christmas and on this place. I can't wait to get back to work and some peace and civility.'

'And I want—' said Mel from under the table

'*Oh, shut up, Mel!*' said everyone.

3
Elf

The scree trickled between their feet like money through the fingers of a miser: a tumble of broken rock, like a waterfall frozen into shards of grey ice. But as they reached the first crest, there were bigger, brighter boulders, puddles of green grass, and leggy, fragile flowers flickering in the vestige of a breeze. Climbing made them sweat and pant, and the air was so hot that breathing it in seemed to fuel their sweating. So they climbed and sat, climbed and sat, taking all morning to reach the top of Third Wrinkle. Mr Shepherd had seen no joy in such a sweltering excursion, and had stayed in the bedroom reading his paper. Mel and his mother had given up climbing, to picnic and play on a safe, flat area half-way up. Only Joy and Holly had pressed on higher.

Oh, but it was worth it! The drought had reduced the dry upland to moonscapes while, here and there, the lakes and spring-fed streams made for brilliant green oases of grass shimmering silver in the sunlight. Almost like snow.

'I should've gone to the cash-and-carry with Dad,' said Holly, spread-eagling herself on the steep slope like a starfish on the side of a blue pool.

'Your mum didn't seem to mind you bringing us up here.'

'Well, she wouldn't say if she did, would she? Your mum asked. Always oblige the customers. That's the rule. When you need the money, you have to be obliging.' She made it sound like having to eat frogs with a fork. Joy did not say so but 'obliging' was not the word that sprang to mind in connection with Mrs Partridge.

Still, she *had* made them all picnic lunches; Holly had carried Joy's all the way up the Wrinkle in her rucksack. Unfortunately, that was not all she had carried. Tipping the bag out onto the dry, crisp grass, a big stone fell out, too. She had picked it up at the bottom of the fell, and crammed it in on top of the sandwiches. It had squashed them into one thin, white, damp pancake. Taking the rock in two hands now, she climbed further up, to the very highest knoll and to a heap of similar rocks, where she let it fall with a loud crack.

'What's that? A cairn?' called Joy.

'Nope. I'm turning the mountain upside down,' Holly said as she skidded back down. 'Every time I come up here, I bring a stone from the bottom. If I live long enough—or if my children and their children go on doing it, gradually the bottom will get moved to the top and the top to the bottom.' She said it as though it were the most sensible project anyone could undertake, and when she saw Joy look at her strangely, she just shrugged, unsmiling and unrepentant. 'At least it will confuse the geologists a couple of hundred years from now.'

Far below, the lake sweated drops of sunlight. It was easy to imagine the passage of centuries in such a place.

Forever Xmas was still plainly visible far below, its absurd number of chimneys bristling like the legs of an overturned beetle. The top of each stack was sealed off with a cowling, to keep birds from nesting. A major obstacle to Father Christmas, too, thought Joy, envisaging at the base of each chimney the pristine grate, the Christmas-decked room, the odd, unseasonal Christmassers.

'The Japanese are leaving,' she observed sleepily, watching a group of tiny figures push their suitcases out to a taxi, like ants rolling seeds towards a winter nest.

'Good,' said the elf. 'Dad doesn't like the Japanese. At least, he thinks he shouldn't. He and Mum, they're into the Second World War in a big way. The music, the clothes, you know. Born out of their time, really. Should've been born twenty years earlier, when all the movies were great and men wore hats and comfortable trousers. No one's nose ran when they cried . . . In point of fact, he liked them a lot—the Japanese girls, I mean. They laughed a lot, which is more than you can say for anyone else we've got just now.'

'Who are the others?' asked Joy, though she didn't really expect Holly to know. It was business; why should she? Holly just happened to live there.

But Holly did know. This pale, sunless elf, sent dipping into the dreams and belongings of her mother's guests, had developed quite an art for reckoning up the lives of those who invaded her home. 'Right now, there's Mr Oil-Well— Halliwell, in fact. He's the big bully on Table 4. Works on an oil rig; earns a pile of money. Leaves his wife to run a nice orderly household, then comes barging back every few months creating havoc, throwing his money around, trying to get back in with the kids.

'There's good old Aunty Sheel, the glam Australian on Number 1. She's visiting her long-lost nieces and remembering why she went to all that trouble to emigrate and get away from them.

'Then there's the Strangers. You know? On Table 6? Mr L'Estrange and Offspring? We get a lot like him. Parents divorced. The children spend Christmas with their mum, so Dad brings them here to get his turn. Spends all his time slanging off the mother. Trying to sow the seeds, so they'll go home hating her as much as he does. Trying to win them over to his side in the war.'

'You don't think much of people, do you?' said Joy, feeling some part of her recoil from Holly Partridge, so shrewd and so shrewish towards her fellow human beings.

'What do you mean? I think about them all the time! What else is there to think about round here?' Her bitterness

18

suddenly melted like a pocketful of toffee. 'I mean, I wish I knew what to think about Table 3. That sad Mr Starr. That sad boy of his. They love each other—you can see that much straight off, just looking at them. But it's all gone wrong somehow. Something strange there. Worrying.' And Joy saw all at once that Holly had brought them up the fellside with her, as surely as she had carried the rock: sad Mr Starr and his boy.

'What did they wish for?' she asked, trying to be helpful.

Holly emerged, with a struggle, from her train of thought. 'I don't know. They never filled in the forms. Came by taxi, not car. And they've got no luggage to go through; nothing to speak of.'

'*You go through people's luggage!*' Joy gasped.

It was said more in awe than disapproval, but Holly realized that she had given away more than she should, and pulled her knees up to her chest. 'Some people are more interesting than others,' she said defensively. Bright spots of colour glowed in the hollows of her white cheeks.

Joy felt she should change the subject. 'What about us, then? Us Shepherds.'

The elf got up rather sharply, looped the strap of the empty bag over her head, and moved off, without actually looking at Joy. 'Oh, *you*,' she said with exaggerated flippancy. 'You don't count. You only came here by accident. You're the original Happy Family, aren't you? Not a cloud in your sky. You don't fit in here. Far too hunky-dory.'

Joy got up and followed her—over the brow of the Wrinkle—to be met by the merest breeze and the full splendour of Cold Pike. It reared up before them, a tidal wave of rock petrified to stillness by some palaeolithic sight too horrible to endure. Here and there, on its vertical flank, Joy could make out pitons and tufts of rope left in its side by climbers, as harpoons are left in the flanks of undefeated whales.

At some time—maybe ten years, maybe one thousand—huge chunks of the overhang had fallen away, crashing down and embedding themselves in deep craters on the brow of Third Wrinkle—pockmarks fifteen feet deep, which grass and time had softened into a series of bowl-like depressions. Graceless and ruthless, the cliff walled in the valley of Wasthwaite, denying access to the neighbouring landscape. Its base blocked their path. In fact it was a cliff from which every footpath turned back. Holly Partridge, for all her ambitions to turn mountains upside down, could never have strayed further than this, this buttress of impassible rock, even when she did manage to escape the big white house with its sealed chimneys.

And what about you? thought Joy as she followed the elf back down the sheep tracks of Third Wrinkle. Skivvying all hours. Slaving away for your parents. Sharing your home with strangers. What about you and *your* happy family? It seemed to Joy that the Partridges, by Holly's own criterion, were well suited to Forever Xmas, a place where discontented people came looking for happiness out of season.

By the time they got back to the house, a new guest had arrived, and other worries besides.

'*Where were you? What kept you?*' Holly's mother greeted her daughter, in a whisper clearly audible to Joy as she struggled on the stairs with the first of the fire-doors. Mrs Partridge had hold of her daughter by the biceps and was shaking her with the vehemence of her own panic. 'I've had the police on the phone . . . It gave me such a scare. Listen,' and she drew the elf away, like a lioness dragging its prey to a tree to eat at leisure.

Poor girl, thought Joy, recalling a wealth of fairy stories; Cinderella, Gretel, Snow White.

The new guest was a mystery: a man of about forty, all on his own. The Shepherds saw him at dinnertime, sitting with one elbow on the table, reading the menu. He read the front of it (the meal), the back of it (the drinks) and then his plate (front and back), his glass, his fork and knife and spoon. The look on his face was of a university professor confronted with a particularly puerile comic. He kept shaking his head in exaggerated bewilderment. When his melon arrived, his top lip rolled up to mimic the slice of dry ham pinned to the fruit with a cocktail stick. He was dapper—almost good-looking, with curly blond hair and a face like El Greco used to paint— an elongated oval full of anguish. So what was he doing there, on his own?

Joy watched Holly, restored to her green elf costume, go over and invite him to take his coffee through to the games room where Mr Partridge was about to play the piano for a Christmas sing-song. He gave her a look of thinly concealed contempt, and said he would drink his coffee where he was, thank you.

'So *tonight* is it Christmas?' Mel was saying, mixing spray cream into his chocolate mousse.

'Not for us,' said his mother crisply.

'Well, is it *tomorrow*, then?' His whine grew shriller.

'Perhaps. We'll see.' Mrs Shepherd was in a quandary. The broken car still did not reappear, and she was half inclined to abandon good sense and leap into the yawning chasm of pretend-Christmas.

Red glimpses of Santa Claus crossing the yard, climbing the stairs, drinking tea beyond the swing doors to the kitchen were exciting Mel to a frenzy of hope. 'I'll be good, really I will!' he pleaded, cocking his head so far over in an effort to engage his mother's eyes that his fine hair lifted.

'It isn't that, dear . . . ' She looked to her husband for help, but he kept the paper raised in front of his face and shook it irritably. He had already negotiated a discount with Mr Partridge for *not* having filled stockings delivered to the room and an audience with Santa.

'Oh, take him through and do some singing, will you?' she told Joy. But Mel did not want to go, not without securing a promise of Christmas. Not until the elf, in her creased green satin and bright elfin smile, came looking for carol singers did he clamber to his feet on the chair and ask to be picked up.

Surliness and resentment were nowhere to be seen in Holly's face now. She was full of hilarity and fun, bouncing Mel on her hip as if she had carried dozens of children over the stony acres of their small sorrows. She was in the mood for confidences, too.

'Did you see him?' she whispered to Joy. 'His name's Angel! All on his own, and he's booked two nights. The police phoned today, to say there's a man absconded from the open prison in Keswick and to watch out for him. Mum got herself in a terrible state thinking we'd come face to face with him on the mountainside and got ourselves murdered and buried in shallow graves. Then this weirdo turned up on the doorstep, and she had *him* down as the gaolbird— Mr Angel! Poor Mum. The perils of an anxious nature.'

'Could he be?' said Joy uneasily. 'Could Mr Angel be the escaped convict?'

'Oh, come on! Where do you think you are? *Great Expectations*? Maroons firing on the marshes? Shaven-headed men in manacles, jumping out from behind tombstones? For one thing, they don't put mass murderers in open prisons. And for another, Angel dresses like a Mormon and drives a Mondeo. Of course he's not a . . . ' She broke off from what she was saying, as a stray thought distracted her—much as a cat might glance up from its dinner to watch a mouse go by. Then she tickled Mel till he squealed and slithered out of her

22

arms. 'There are worse things, of course,' she said, but only to herself.

As she drew the sliding doors apart which separated the dining room from the 'parlour', the noise of singing hit them like water from a sluice gate. Mr Partridge was a slight, smooth-skinned man with large wrist-bones, ginger hair like crushed velvet and the startled expression of a fox newly hit by a car. His piano was a Yamaha keyboard and had a bright synthesized 4/4 shug-a-tugging beat hissing out beneath the melody.

' . . . *sorrowing, sighing, bleeding, dying, Sealed in the stone-cold tomb!*' bellowed Mr Halliwell the oil-rig man, an open can of lager in one hand and a carol sheet in the other. His son was playing with a Game Boy, while his daughter crumbled crisps into the small fish tank on the sideboard. The L'Estrange children were being introduced to alcoholic lemonade because their mother would not have approved, and the father and son—the ones who had no luggage to speak of—sat quietly in a corner, tears sparkling on the boy's lashes.

Mel tugged on the hem of Holly's green satin. She squatted down, eyes bright with interest, to hear what Mel had to say.

'Is he really?' said Mel.

'Is who—?'

'An angel,' said Mel, almost silently, because he was holding his breath. 'Is he really an angel, do you s'pose?'

4
Angel

They told him no, but the idea lodged in Mel's mind. Already disorientated by meeting Christmas in the middle of August, he was further agitated by the wonder being withheld. It was there, in the house, and yet he was not allowed to reach out and grab it. On the first morning, he looked out of his window and saw Santa Claus in a red T-shirt, feeding the chickens. Despite beating on the windows he could not make the old man look up, so tried to run downstairs to him. But like a fly trapped in a jamjar he had just ricocheted helplessly between fire-doors too heavy for him to open.

He felt the same frustration every time he spoke to his mother. Was there to be a Christmas? Time and again she fobbed him off: 'Maybe tomorrow'; 'Ask your father'. And his father only snarled behind his newspaper. All around them, people were having Christmas—bright, sparkly, painted metal-and-plastic, light-flashing, siren-wailing Christmas careering between the ketchup and the salt. But not him. What had he done wrong, he asked himself, to be denied it, to be shunned by the man in red, to be barred from the cupboard under the stairs where he had *seen* stuffed stockings hanging.

So he wished. Closing his eyes and fists as tight as the spring in an overwound toy, he wished spitefully for his father's car to perish, to die, to be consumed by the fire and smoke that had brought them here. It was a curse so terrible that it made his diaphragm quake and his teeth chatter. That night, he dreamed that he saw the car mobbed by flocks of

24

black birds which pecked out its headlamps and flayed its wheels of their rubber.

The garage had done its best: the spare part, they said, would take at least one day to come. They had made time for Christmas to happen. And still his father talked of leaving, the moment the car was fixed. In fact Mel perfectly well understood that his father had fixed things with the Partridge woman so that there would be no Christmas for Mel; Christmas for everyone else, but not for him. And he racked his brains for the crime that had condemned him to this outer darkness. The greatest wickedness that came to mind was the Curse itself, and he dared not repeat it.

But now, perhaps, his redemption had arrived. An angel sat eating at the next table, slept in the room at the end of the corridor—Mr Angel, with yellow hair and a shiny car, newly descended from the cosmos into this hot country of Christmas. Perhaps, after all, wishing had been the wrong way to go about things. Prayer was the answer.

And so Mel prayed, locking his fingers into a union so strong that his knuckles cracked. Whether the prayer would be heard by God, by Father-Christmas-of-the-chickens, or by Mr Angel in his hotel bedroom, Mel neither knew nor cared. He knew only the power of it, surging out of him in devout waves of longing—'Make it Christmas. Make it Christmas. Make it be Christmas!'

Mel could not sleep at bedtime, but Mr Angel haunted that space between wakefulness and slumber, swooping on outstretched wings of feathery gold along corridors of collapsing ice. When he woke next morning, he could not remember whether or not Mr Angel existed. Then, at breakfast, he saw him, and went and stared (as Isaiah must have done in the smoky Temple), stared at the seraphim eating a boiled egg. The material delights of Christmas almost melted away in the heat of that marvellous moment. The notion

25

dazzled Mel Shepherd's soul: that an angel should be sniffing a boiled egg not two paces away, sniffing each spoonful in turn.

'Do you want something?' said Mr Angel.

'*Yes, please!*' said Mel reverently.

Mr Angel curved his hands protectively round his breakfast plate and scowled. 'What exactly?'

'Oh, *anything*,' said Mel in a whisper choked with emotion.

Mr Angel scraped margarine over a slice of toast and held it out towards Mel with a mixture of distaste and worry. Mel took the toast and ate it, without really noticing: adults were always thrusting food at him. Still he stood and stared, worshipping.

'All right, then,' said Mr Angel, increasingly uncomfortable. 'You've got what you came for. Off you go to your . . . *pseudo* Christmas.'

The little boy turned and ran full-tilt across the dining room, his face hot and red, crashing into chairs, falling over and picking himself up. He scrambled up into his chair and began attacking his breakfast with a ruthless, exultant joy. He did not know what pseudo meant: 'longed for', 'prayed for' presumably, but he knew that Christmas would soon be his. An angel had granted it. When he picked up a rasher of bacon and sniffed it, and his father told him that was no way to eat, Mel retorted, 'It's how *angels* eat.'

Sniff, sniff, sniff. Fondly, Joy watched her little brother sniff each morsel of his breakfast in turn, and wondered vaguely where he got his strange ideas from and whether she had been the same at his age. For reasons of her own, she too glanced furtively round at the mysterious Mr Angel. But Mr Angel was no longer sniffing his food. He seemed to be putting it into an array of small plastic bags laid out in front of him on the table. A tomato, an egg yolk, a slice of bacon . . . When he had done so, he put them into an attaché case and got up to go.

Joy stood up so fast that she spilled her cereal.

'Oh, for God's sake . . . !' said her father, instantly enraged as he always was by spills.

She knew she ought to stay and clear up the mess, but there was no time. Even now, Holly Partridge was in Mr Angel's room trying to find out who he was and why he had come. His order of a full English breakfast had suggested she would have plenty of time. But apparently he had not wanted to eat it, only to bag it. Even so, if Joy could reach the stairs before him, she might just be in time to warn Holly.

'Come back here at once, Joy Shepherd, and clear up this mess!'

But she chose not to hear—dodged out into the hall and along to the pay phone. She had just picked it up when Mr Angel emerged, his briefcase clutched to his chest.

'Telephone call for you, Mr Angel,' she said, thrusting the receiver at him. And while he stood questioning the dead phone—'Hello? Hello?'—Joy bounded on up the glass-walled staircase, like a fish surfacing in an aquarium. Breathless, she reached the top floor and the door of Angel's room. She beat with her fist below the number 7. There was a noise like scuttling rats inside, but Holly did not open the door.

Joy could hear Angel's footsteps on the stairs now, see the top of his head rising into view. In a moment he would turn the corner and see her. '*Too late!*' she hissed through the door, then retreated down the corridor towards her own room, brushing shoulders with Mr Angel on the way.

'Was that a joke?' he asked with frosty hauteur.

'What?' said Joy with a guilty start, banging her shoulder against a fire extinguisher.

'The phone call.'

'No, sir. Of course not, sir,' said Joy. 'There was a woman . . .'

He looked her over for a moment with supercilious scepticism, then continued on to his room. Joy stopped in her bedroom doorway, waiting to hear a shout of rage as he walked in on the elf rifling through his belongings.

His key rattled in the lock, then the door shut with a thud. But there was no shout. Joy craned her head into the corridor, staring after him.

'I got out through the window,' said a voice so close behind her that Joy jumped with fright. 'There's a tree.' It was Holly. She had come round the house, up the fire escape and in at the window of the Shepherd's room. 'Thanks for the warning.'

That was when Joy felt the first thrill and companionship of a shared adventure. It forged friendship out of acquaintance. She knew she had changed, in Holly's eyes, from a guest into a friend, and for some reason that seemed a privilege . . . though she could not quite say why, given the peculiar, down-trodden surliness of this care-worn elf. 'Well? What did you find out? What is he doing here?'

'Nothing. There's nothing. A change of suit. A washbag. No photographs of a wife or children. No camera. No guides. No reporter's notebook. I thought he might just be a travel journalist—or someone checking out the B & Bs for a guide-book. You know: *Weekends away in the Lake District*, that sort of thing.' There were large circles of sweat darkening her elf costume, and rust stains on her tights off the fire escape. 'Just what we need. A mention. A bit in one of the Sundays.'

'It might be in his briefcase,' Joy suggested. 'The notebook—along with his breakfast.' And she described the plastic bags.

But instead of reassurance, the elf registered instant dismay. 'Damn!' she said. 'Oh damn, damn, damn, damn!' She clenched her fists and she ducked her head, and she burst into sudden, desolate tears.

Joy put her arms around her—could not think what else to do to muffle her noise.

At that moment, little Mel burst in at the bedroom door having struggled up all the stairs to bring his sister the great news. 'We can have Christmas!' he yelled. 'Mum says we can have Christmas!'

'Put down mouse-traps, mother, and clean the cooker!'

Holly flung open the fridge and began groping around inside it, pulling things to the front. 'What's this?'

'Mayonnaise, dear,' said Mrs Partridge. 'What else would it be?'

'What's it made of?'

'F.C.'s eggs, of course. Fresh out of the barn.'

There was no Christmas in the kitchen; it was the first thing Joy noticed. No decorations, no candles: nothing but the smell.

'Throw it away. Get rid of it, I've told you before: no eggs. You can't use real eggs any more. It's the regulations.'

Instead of seasonal jingles, a tape recorder in the corner was playing Big Band music on strident trumpets.

'Where's your hat?' said Holly to her mother. 'Those paper bath-hat things, the ones we got at the cash-and-carry?'

'I've got my net on. I always have my net.'

'Nets don't count any more, Mum!'

Mrs Partridge quailed visibly from her daughter's uproar. Joy, half-in and half-out of the swing doors, wanted to go, get away, go back to the cheerfulness of Mel. But how much of a friend would she be to Holly if she did not help avert this obvious disaster? Whatever it was.

In fact she found she still had hold of Mel's hand and that he too was leaning into the kitchen watching Holly slam cupboard doors.

'Can I do anything?' Joy asked nervously.

'It's Angel,' said Holly. 'He's Environmental Health. If he finds one speck of dirt, one mouse dropping, one slice of corned beef in with the raw turkey, he can close us down!'

Mrs Partridge gave a wail. Mr Partridge swore softly under his breath. They were both galvanized into a look of imminent action, elbows out, hands at the ready . . . but too unnerved actually to move. Holly raced round them, opening drawers, examining utensils. Like the lone defender of a besieged castle she prepared to defend her home from the onslaught of Angel and all his hosts.

'Dad, check all the fire-doors are shut. Halliwell keeps propping them open with the fire extinguishers. Mum, F.C.'s chicken feed has got to go out of the larder. He mustn't keep it in here.'

Joy watched mesmerized. Was this her supposed Cinderella, the down-trodden scullery maid, the one she had thought needed rescuing from parental neglect and cruelty? Was this the poor exploited creature sent like a Victorian chimney-sweep into the fire-grates of Forever Xmas, to do her mother's dirty-work? Joy began to sense she had misread the situation.

'Mum, that plaster on your finger.'

'I burned myself, dear. I'm sorry.'

'It ought to be blue. Take it off or change it for a blue one. I told you: only blue plasters in the kitchen, in case they drop in the food.'

Mel looked up at his sister, bewildered. 'Do blue plasters taste better?' he whispered. He had begun to pick up on the sense of prevailing fright, and to tremble. The pudding on the stove boiled over with a hiss, and everyone jumped.

Just then, Holly's grandfather came in from the garden, making big muddy footmarks on the floor with his fell boots. He was wearing his pyjama jacket unbuttoned, and red Santa

30

Claus trousers with the braces hanging down to his knees. He unwound a rope from a figure-of-eight hook on the wall and lowered, into the midst of them, a ceiling rack hung with drying washing. One of Mr Partridge's shirts sprawled across the kitchen table. Grandpa Partridge helped himself to a clean red T-shirt and stripped off his pyjama jacket.

'There's a spy in the camp, F.C.,' said Holly. 'Come to check up on us all. See that we're doing things right.'

'Well?' said Grandpa struggling into the shirt. 'Aren't we?'

Holly softened like a punctured balloon. All the shrillness went out of her, and she sat down on a kitchen chair as if to catch her breath. A tentative smile came back to her face. 'Yes. Yes. Why am I panicking?' she said. 'We don't poison anyone, do we? We never poisoned anyone. We've got nothing to hide, have we?'

Her mother and father also sat down, mopping their brows as if the enemy had just ridden on past the fort.

'You like to panic. Your mother always loved a good panic. *Hakuna matata*, I say. Eh, boy? *Hakuna matata*.' As his head emerged from the T-shirt, Grandpa Partridge had noticed Mel wriggling fully into the kitchen to gaze at him. The shirt was an old-style Liverpool football strip. The initial L had been unpicked from the breast pocket to leave only the letters F.C.

'My mum says we can have Christmas,' said Mel. He meant to say it to Mrs Partridge who, he knew, was in charge of such things. But his eyes would not, could not leave the white hair, the blue eyes that transfixed him.

The old man looked him over appraisingly. 'That's good. Better come with me, then. Do you like chickens, boy? Give the boy a packet of crisps, mother.' And slipping one of the braces over his shoulder, he gave Mel the other to hold, cantering out of the kitchen door whistling the theme from *The Lion King*. They speeded up to a gallop as they went down

31

the garden path, a thin ungainly scarlet reindeer and his small sleigh driver.

Mel knew this was the real one. In his short life he had already met a dozen—at nursery school, in shops, at garden centres, on special Santa trains. But looking back, Mel knew full well they had not been the real thing: mere look-alikes standing in for someone too busy, in the run-up to Christmas, to be wasting his time in provincial garden centres or riding trains up and down a branch line. *Here* was the real one. After all, Mel had summoned him by the power of prayer.

This one did not depend upon a red suit, a white beard. This one did not say ho ho ho! for want of conversation. This one did not confine himself to dark, unlit places to flatter a tacky disguise. This one was nothing like people imagined— not fat or bearded or chortling, but whippet thin, with protruding ribs and collar bones, and a lily-white skin stark against the sunburn of his arms and neck. He scattered all Mel's preconceptions: real life always does.

Of course he had shaved off his beard: in a heatwave, who wouldn't? Of course he slept in pyjamas rather than in a fur-trimmed jacket and wellington boots. To see him off-duty only increased the man's magic. For there was no denying—in costume or out of it—this old man was the embodiment of Christmas. It was in his walk. It was embroidered on his shirt. Above all, it was in his eyes: a vague, detached chaos; a childlike anarchy, a riot of implausible possibilities.

Not for him the sudden dissolution on Twelfth Night, like Cinderella's coach disintegrating round her on the stroke of twelve. Here was more than a twelve-day wonder. This and a thousand other childish intuitions told Mel that he was in the company of the true, the real, the genuine Father Christmas.

'Come and see my bantams, boy,' said F.C., dragging open the barn door. 'If you can find any eggs, they're yours. Not a fox, are you? Not a rat or a stoat, are you? Got a secret to show you. Don't tell, will you?'

Watching from the house, Joy saw them disappear into the dark. Her heart had sunk when F.C. walked into the kitchen. Now Mel would realize that Santa was only Holly's grandpa, dressed up. But either he did not associate the old man with the scarlet figure glimpsed around the hotel, or else 'F.C.' had managed to remain convincing even without his costume beard. For she could hear Mel laughing, hooting with laughter. For a moment she thought she saw his happiness burst the confines of the big black barn and come spilling out, feathery and white, but it was only the bantam chickens leaping out into the sunshine.

Fleetingly she was jealous, excluded from this treat which had been extended to Mel, but not, of course, to her. She was too old. Too old for rhinestone grottos. Too old for games of pretend. Too old to believe in flying reindeer and elastic chimneys. These days, being the older sister, she was supposed to derive her pleasure from watching Mel's; a last twinge of childish pique went through her like an earth tremor.

Then the barn door suddenly swung wide, and more chickens spilled out ahead of a large green motor mower. The mower was being driven, erratically and fast, by an old man in braces and red underwear. Standing up between his knees, on the juddering rusty petrol tank, holding a clutch of eggs and a handful of the old man's hair, was Mel, his shriek of joy shaken into a machine-gun stutter by the vibration. Up and down the dead, brown lawn they rode, grazing the paintwork on the rockery, knocking over the bird bath and singing 'Jingle Bells' at the tops of their voices.

5

Three Wise Men

'I've got a place where I go,' said F.C. to Mel. 'Want to come?'

'The North Pole?' said Mel, wiping the mower oil off his hands on to his trousers.

'Nah. Damnable cold place. Full of bears: kill you soon as look at you. Cracks opening up to fall in. Cold like a pick-axe. We old sorts don't like the cold. Nor the ice. Brittle bones, sithee? Broken hip and that's it for us. Pneumonia. Shedfuls of pneumonia up there. At the North Pole. And no birds. Only ptarmigans maybe. Ptarmigans. Pneumonia. Lots of silent P's, sithee? Lots of silence altogether. I like silence. But I like birds better. You like birds, boy? I could show you birds round here you've never seen where you come from. Where do you come from? Buzzards. Kestrel. Twite. Ravens. If the heat slacks off, I'll take you up there. To my special place. Agreed? It's up there.' And he pointed at the crest of the Third Wrinkle—beyond it, perhaps, to Cold Pike.

'Let's go now!' said Mel, grasping the old man's hand, trying to drag him towards the mountain.

'Nay. Too hot, too hot. You come to my *other* special place. My den. My lair. You can tell me what you want out of life.'

They turned back towards the house. The sun was above the roof. F.C. shaded his eyes against it and waved to someone at an upstairs window, a flicker of green. Mel recognized the elf and waved too. But Holly was not looking out at them. She was peering intently beyond them, over their

34

heads and away down the long drive, at the dust of an approaching car.

'Joy! Have you seen the Starrs?' hissed Holly.

Joy had been organized into playing Twister with the L'Estrange children and the Australian's nieces. The elf squatted down beside the sheet of spotted plastic.

'In the sky, d'you mean?'

'The Starrs, idiot. Mr Starr and his boy.'

'Ursa Major and Ursa Minor,' mused Joy who was poised, like the Clifton Suspension Bridge, over a tangle of sweaty bodies. 'Have you tried their room?' The L'Estrange girl lurched up underneath her and pressed a hip into a stomach full of breakfast. The heat was terrible—a thundery, headaching heat made their sweaty fists slip on the plastic. Like eels they knotted and slithered over one another, too uncomfortable to laugh. The Gordion knot collapsed in a heap, and Joy squirmed free. 'Why?' She could tell it was important. Holly was flushed and breathless.

'They're not in their room. Come and help me look. Please. I have to find them. Now.'

Outside the sunny windows, a blue flashing light competed with the feeble blinking of the Christmas tree lights indoors. A car door slammed.

'I know where they'll be,' said Joy. 'Table football. In the basement. They're into table football, those two.'

So Holly and Joy tripped down the steps to what had once been the coal hole and which now contained table football, ping-pong, and a broken slot machine. Mr Starr and his son were playing, face-to-face across the footballers, thrashing at the row of handles, laughing so loud and making such a clatter that they did not even hear the footsteps on the stairs. Joy realized it was the first time she had heard anything from

35

them but hushed murmurings, the only time she had seen them laugh.

'Mr Starr, Mr Starr!' said Holly. 'F.C. would like to see Ronnie now. Can you both come? Please? Straight away?'

Mr Starr was a smart man gone to seed, like a neglected gooseberry bush, leggy with small, gooseberry-coloured eyes. He had been good-looking once, but worry seemed to have worn out his face, a hereditary worry that was already reshaping the features of his son. Starr shot a look of rank mistrust at Holly, then quickly glancing back at his boy asked, 'Want to? Do you want to visit Father Christmas?'

The boy pulled a face and shook his head, too old at nine for such childishness.

'*I really think you should,*' said Holly, loud and deliberate, as if to a foreigner. Joy could not fathom it. Was it a rule of the house? 'The police are in the hall,' Holly added, and both father and son jolted as if an electric current had passed through the red moulded grips of the football table. The footballers froze in mid-game. The ball rolled slowly down the sloping table and in at a goalmouth with a bang which brought another rolling into play. Then, with a flurry of brisk jollity, Holly flapped her hands at the pair. 'Come on. Come on. I'll show you the way. Nothing to worry about. He's very nice. You can tell him anything. He can *keep a secret*. He's good at *keeping secrets*.'

Ronnie Starr did not seem able to let go of the grips. His father had to circle the table and pick him up, clasping the big boy to his chest and looking around him for any belongings they might have brought down to the games room. 'Why should you care?' he asked.

Holly said nothing but began resolutely back up the stairs. Joe Starr stumbled after her, shielding his son's head against the low lintel. 'Why should she help us?' he asked Joy, who was forced to bring up the rear.

Joy didn't know. She was only just working out who he was, let alone why Holly should want to help him. She knew that you were not supposed to talk to strangers, in case they were criminal. Presumably that meant you were definitely not supposed to talk to criminals . . .

In the hall, two men in suits, looking distressed by the heat, were showing Mr Partridge a photograph. He was still holding the spinner from the game of Twister and his forefinger idly spun the arrow round and round and round.

'If you could look at it carefully . . . Our enquiries lead us to believe he may have rendezvoused with his son in this vicinity. A brochure was found . . . ' A uniformed constable strolled in from the car park.

'A brochure, oh. One of ours? Oh,' said Mr Partridge. He looked down at the photograph, whirling the plastic arrow, saying nothing. 'You could look at our books. You won't find there's anyone by that name . . . '

His wife came out of the kitchen with flour on her hands. 'What is it, Colin?'

'The police, dear. About that prisoner. Out of Keswick. Seems he might not be on his own, after all. Might be his son's missing, too.' Ivy Partridge glanced over her husband's shoulder, still preoccupied with matters of health and safety, no longer fearful that Mr Angel was the hunted man: the truth about Mr Angel was quite bad enough.

But when she saw the face in the photograph, she made a noise like a dog stepped on. 'Oh no. Oh no, it couldn't be. Not him. Not nice Mr . . . It is, isn't it, Colin? It's Mr Starr. Oh, my lord. Oh, my good God.' She gripped her husband's arm with floury hands. Fragments of bacon stuck to his sleeve.

'I suppose it does look a *little* like him,' said Mr Partridge. 'I haven't got my glasses on, of course,'

The police exchanged looks of mutual congratulation, and began to speak in energetic, clipped undertones. 'Where are they now? We'll take over. Nothing to worry about.'

'Oh, my good God, Colin! Here, in this house! . . . I don't know where. Where are they, Colin? Where would they be? Were they playing Twister with you?' The idea of a criminal intertwined with her law-abiding guests was almost too much for Mrs Partridge to contemplate without sitting down, and she plumped down on the hall chair. The angel chimes turned faster in the breeze from the open front door—an alarum of tinkling.

'No, no, I haven't seen them all morning,' said Mr Partridge.

'Check the room,' said the senior detective. 'We'll be needing a key, sir. Have you got a key?' And leaving the uniformed officer by the door, they thumped upstairs, bent on an early and easy arrest.

'I thought when you rang . . . ' Mrs Partridge's voice carried down the stairwell, 'I naturally thought . . . a man on his own . . . I never—Well, how would I?'

A through-draught set the double kitchen doors gaping, and a catflap rapped, even though the Partridges had no cat.

The willow tree gushed out of the ground like a fountain, creating a shimmering dome of green and fractured sunlight which cascaded almost to the ground. It was a great green crinoline, a wickiup of leaves, a bell enclosing a clamour of reverberating dark. Under its awning, beside the trunk, seated on mossy, wet ground, it was cool in the dense, dark dapple—like being underwater. Mel leaned against F.C.'s chest and explained what he wanted from life: to be as old as his sister, to ride to school on a tractor, to be able to skip, to grow a beard, to fly.

It was not a shopping list. F.C. listened, but not like a shopkeeper totting up the bill, nor like a magician, wand poised to grant wishes. He listened and nodded, as if he had found the same or similar things lacking from his own life.

'Flying, yes,' he said. 'Though the wings would have to be on a harness. Uncomfortable at night else. Wouldn't care to roost. I like my bed right enough.'

In fact, Mel was purposely withholding his request, recalling how that part always came last—at the garden centre, on the Santa Special Steamer—the request always came last. And he was enjoying himself too much to speed the moment when F.C. would send him back indoors to his mother. So he savoured his request, nursed it like a pain, so great was his faith that F.C. would ultimately grant it.

Through the swaying skirt of the golden willow, they could see pixels of brown grass and white house, the dark green of the Christmas trees planted round the lawn. 'Can anyone see us in here?' asked Mel.

'Nay, lad. It's like an ambulance. See out but not in.'

'I was never in an ambulance.'

'You keep it that way, son. You keep it like that.' As if reminded of some recent ambulance ride, F.C. patted at his pocket. 'I've left my pills in the house.' But he did not stir. A big bumble bee buzzed in and out of the fronded willow tips, feeding on clover in the grass. A bird was bathing in the water butt beside the black barn. 'Building up to thunder, I reckon,' said F.C. 'Hotter every minute. This weather is wearing me away.'

'Are you ill, Father Christmas?'

'Who, me, boy? Where would the world be then, if I got ill?'

'You could always magic yourself better, couldn't you?'

F.C. ruffled his hair and laughed silently, so that Mel's head bounced up and down on his chest. The little boy could feel himself falling asleep, dropping through space, under a green parachute. Strange, when there was so much still to say . . . F.C. nodded off, too, and they cracked heads, waking each other with a start.

'So when are you having Christmas, littl'un?' said F.C.

'After one more sleep.'

'Tomorrow?'

'Yes. Our car is mended nearly. Dad wants to go, right after. I don't. I want to see your secret place. On the mountain.'

'Leaving tomorrow? Bye! Then you'd best tell me what you're hoping I'll bring you.'

There was no more thought of Power Rangers or Mr Muscle, or Megazords or chocolate. Here was magic too powerful for pettiness. Here was an audience with a worker of real miracles. Mel had something much more important in mind: an animal, a live thing, a living creature, a *pet* . . .

But just as Mel was about to unburden his soul of its gigantic wish, the green fronds parted and the elf pushed the Starr boy through the waterfall of greenery, into the dark atrium. His father stumbled in too, eyes unable to adjust at first to the profound shadow.

'F.C., this is Ronnie and his dad. It's Ronnie's turn to talk to you.'

'No it's not!' said Mel, glaring at the Starr boy. But no one listened.

'They're in trouble, F.C. People are looking for them. But they'll be all right here, with you, won't they?' She crouched down, so as to engage her grandfather's eyes. She spoke to him slowly and deliberately, as if to a child, though it was hardly patronizing, for she appeared to be entrusting to him some vitally important task only he could fulfil.

'Go away!' Mel told the Starr boy. 'It's my turn.' But nobody listened.

The old man seemed to struggle for a moment to differentiate between Holly and the dream into which he had been sliding. Then he nodded and patted her hands, and, sliding Mel off his lap, beckoned Ronnie forward. A tableau formed—a stillness and silence Mel wanted to smash with his fists. 'It's not fair! It's not fair!' But Holly took hold of his wrist and tugged him out through the splatter of leaves, so that the sunlight burst in his face like an explosion. He tried to wriggle free, but his sister was there, too, to take his other wrist and drag him away saying, 'Later, Mel. Later. Ice-cream now. Come and have some nice ice-cream. You can come back later.'

There would be no later! Christmas was just a few hours away and he had failed to tell Santa Claus what he really, truly wanted, had been thwarted by Ronnie Starr, ousted by the elf. Looking back at the willow tree, he could not even glimpse F.C. The foliage screened his lair completely, the sunlight dazzling on the cascade of vivid green.

The Starr's room was empty: not a shoe, not a jacket, not a toothbrush. The police searched the whole hotel at a run, pouncing into rooms and cupboards with such aggressive suddenness that Ivy Partridge gave a little cry each time and put her hand over her heart. 'Oh, lord, Colin,' she said. 'And we've got the British Legion in this afternoon!'

'Looks like they've dipped out,' said the police officer pausing at a bedroom window, staring dolefully across the scorched lawn. The other fingered the Christmas decorations, puzzled by them.

'Reckon they saw us coming,' said the one at the window. 'If they're on foot they haven't got far.' He called down to the uniformed officer in the porch to radio in the news.

'Where's Holly?' Mrs Partridge fretted. 'And what with the

other. Oh, it's all too much. Too much! Have you tried the barn?'

The officers ran to the barn, throwing bales of hay about, breaking eggs, scaring the chickens out into the yard. But all they got for their pains was donkey-dung on their shoes, and straws in their hair. There was no sign of Starr or his son.

They showed the photograph to the other guests, mustering them round the piano like carol-singers. Most said they had never seen the man; the photograph was not a good one and besides, being wholly self-absorbed with their own celebrations, they had paid no attention to the other guests in the dining room. Jack Shepherd shrugged and said he supposed he remembered.

Angel—a man paid to be observant—knew him at once, of course. He threw a sour look at Mrs Partridge which implied this was just the sort of place where escaped convicts would resort. But he could cast no light on where Starr might be now. When a search of every room uncovered neither man nor boy, the police withdrew, frustrated and vexed by the heat, to pace up and down the car park, waiting for back-up.

Desperate to atone for her folly in letting a room to an escaped criminal, Mrs Partridge plied them with glasses of lime-juice, lollies from the freezer, cold turkey sandwiches and her recollections of Starr as a shifty, sullen brute. 'My daughter may have talked to the boy,' she said. 'If I just knew where she was . . . '

'I'm here, Mam,' said Holly strolling round the side of the house. 'What's the matter?'

'Where have you *been*!' exclaimed her mother. 'Thank God *he* hasn't got hold of you. It's that Mr Starr: he's only the escaped prisoner, that's all! He's only run off without paying . . . Where've you *been*?'

'With Joy, here,' said Holly, referring to the girl beside her, without referring to Mel who dangled between them red-faced and grizzling—'It's not fair! It's not fair!' Holly adopted a look of sleepy curiosity, as if rousing herself from the torpor of a sunny afternoon.

Overhead, the air shuddered—not with the expected thunder, but the stuttering roar of a search-helicopter rising into view above Cold Pike. Its rotor blades sliced their puny voices to shreds and set the miniature Christmas trees bobbing. Mrs Partridge's long hair collapsed out of its doughnut-shaped roll and she caught it in one hand.

For the first time, she noticed that her fingers were covered in flour and bacon fat, and remembered that she had not yet put the turkeys on to roast.

6
Starrs over the Stable

Holly held up a sheet of paper. She must have been carrying it about, folded small in a pocket, because it was creased into a mosaic of tiny squares. On the back the misprint glared: *A Letter to Snata.* The police were gone, and those who had deceived them were gathered in the cupboard under the stairs to discover why they had done such a thing.

'I found this up the chimney in Number Three. It's Ronnie Starr's wish,' said Holly. And she passed it to her father who read it and passed it on. From hand to hand it went, the grubby, cyclostyled page; from Mr Partridge to Joy, from Joy to F.C. and back to the elf. The writing on it was in leaky blue ballpoint, clots of superfluous ink lodging like tears in the corners of Ronnie's handwriting. It was an anxious hand, the loops of the O's like tiny eyes shut tight. Here was not the usual list, the string of numbered demands, like terrorists' ultimata: I want, I want, I want. Instead, there was just a single line scrawled across the page.

'*Just my Dad. To Be us Together.*'

It did not take long to read.

'Where are they now?' asked Colin Partridge.

'In the barn,' said Holly. 'Up in the hayloft . . . He's going to go back, you know? He always meant to! He just wanted to spend some time with Ronnie, that's all!' She said it urgently, talking too fast. She was the Starrs' advocate, pleading her defendants' cause, asking for clemency.

'What's he in for?' said F.C. 'What did he do?'

'Swindled some money or something. He's an accountant. You know, something to do with money. Nothing horrible, I swear! Ronnie found our brochure somewhere and sent it to his dad in prison. Couldn't they have Christmas together? Couldn't they meet here if he found his way on the train? It looked so close on the map. Only an inch or two, he thought. Not far for his dad to come. And he came . . . Why not? It's not Ronnie's fault. I thought . . . I thought to myself, it's not Ronnie's fault! He didn't do anything. They just want to be together for a couple of days. That's not so terrible, is it? That's what we're here for, isn't it? For that sort of thing. For granting wishes like that. We're Somewhere Else. We don't have to be like the rest of places. We shouldn't let the kind of things happen here that happen other places. Like getting arrested, like getting dragged off in handcuffs in front of your . . . We should be Somewhere Different, where things like that don't happen!' She spread her hands and drew walls in the air, like an architect describing an ambitious building scheme.

And sitting opposite her, in the crowded cupboard under the stairs, Joy could envisage it too—the cloud-capped towers, the fairy palaces of Holly's imagined world. She who had been dragooned into her parents' business, trapped inside their over-ambitious dream, had taken the idea even more to heart than they had. Unfairly saddled with the day-to-day drudgery of helping out, she had taken upon herself the added burden of trying to make Forever Xmas work—to make it what it claimed to be, to achieve the magic it advertised. Beyond the cynical reality of lottery dice and Sanatogen, there was a perfectly reckless ambition at work in her *not* to be bogus, *not* to be a charlatan. Somewhere along the way, Holly Partridge had appointed herself the guardian of Christmas for the likes of Ronnie Starr.

'Your mother mustn't find out, that's for sure,' said Colin Partridge. 'She's moithered enough already.'

A silence fell filled only by the whirring of the big old electricity meter whose racing white cogwheel indicated that both ovens were working at full capacity.

'And we're quite sure, are we, that the boy's safe?' Colin Partridge worked his way down a mental list of objections. 'Are we sure he's not being held hostage? Hasn't been abducted? I mean, he's quite safe?'

'Oh yes. The boy's safe,' F.C. answered at once. Though his reading glasses magnified his milky blue eyes and gave him a look of vacancy, he remained an expert on certain subjects: he knew the state of a child's heart. However erratic and unpredictable he might seem, he had fully grasped the question in debate: should they go on harbouring an escaped prisoner or tell the police that he was hiding in their barn.

'The police think they're gone—moved on,' said Holly, increasingly eager and optimistic. 'In a couple of days he'll go back to Keswick of his own accord. Won't it look better if he gives himself up of his own free will, rather than getting caught and sent back?' She held the letter close to her chest, the sad little letter, the wish posted by an unbelieving boy to a non-existent Santa.

Just my Dad. To Be us Together.

'What harm can it do? What good are we, if we can't do this one little thing?' Holly singled out her father, directing her words at him alone, knowing that F.C. was already on her side. Her father had to be the one great stumbling block, the timid and law-abiding citizen.

He took the letter from her and read it again, his arms at full stretch, reading glasses in his other jacket. Tears welled on to his lower lashes, then drained away without falling.

It's like this was his own boy, thought Joy, incredulous.

'We're all agreed then, are we?' he said. 'They can stay here, hidden. Just for a couple of days.'

Holly made a triumphant fist. The meter whirred, and clicked up a round thousand therms. F.C. nodded his head and took a pill, to dispel a different kind of heart-ache.

But Joy said, 'No.'

They all stared at her.

'No. It's wrong. It's a crime. Why protect criminals like him? It's wrong.' Still they stared, and Joy flushed scarlet to the roots of her hair. 'It's probably just an excuse anyway. Starr doesn't mean to go back. He wouldn't break out just to see his son. Not just to be with his son. Criminals don't do things like that. Grown ups don't. Fathers don't *do* that kind of thing.'

Joy began to breathe faster. The smallness of the room oppressed her. The ready-filled, stripy, woollen stockings dangling from pegs around all four walls seemed to be kicking at her head, as though she had fallen under a rugby scrum, in among the flailing feet. She got up, banging her head on the low ceiling, and fumbled with the door handle. She had to get out—get out and phone the police, get out and tell her parents, get out and rejoin the real world!

But once in the hall, she ran straight through the open doorway and across the lawn, over to the children's playground where a red tubular frame dangled three kinds of swings and a car tyre. She jumped up on to the swingboat, her feet on the seats, and set it lurching forward and back, forward and back, higher and higher with every jerk of her feet. Sky and grass alternated in her field of vision and, out of the corner of her eye, the black barn. The swing squealed.

After a time, she was aware of the swing alongside hers moving, too. Holly Partridge was sitting on it, scuffing the soles of her old-fashioned sandals. 'He's all right really,' Holly said at last, in a soft, soothing voice. 'I've seen worse. He's OK. Your dad.'

'Who said anything about *my* dad? What's my dad got to do with it? . . . Anyway, how would you know! You don't know anything, you!' Joy retorted, and the swingboat began to pitch again. It did not surprise Joy that the elf should have read her thoughts exactly. Holly knew everything. It was her job, in this odd dysfunctional place, to know everything about everyone. Even what they were thinking.

'Yours has just come a bit . . . detached, that's all. I see it all the time here. It's like that for dads. They get this baby. They think they'll give it the world and ninepence. They work all hours to do that. And they come detached. In the end it's like a lighted window for them; them on the outside looking in. There's the wife and children all cosy and close. And it's as if all the locks have been changed and he can't get his key in the door any more. He's shut out. That's all that's happened to yours.'

In the throes of her rage, Joy hugely resented this calm, reasonable wisdom. It cast her in the role of just another visitor, just another child needing to be made happy by the all-seeing, all-knowing, in-house elf. But quite soon she began to feel seasick from the swinging, and more miserable than angry. 'I thought you said we were so *hunky-dory*, us Shepherds,' she said peevishly, lowering herself down into the boat, letting it rock itself to a standstill.

'I didn't know you properly then; what else would I say? It's not the sort of thing you say to people, is it? "I see you're having a hard time with your dad." . . . Anyway, you're still better off than anyone else here right now. As far as I can see.'

'So you think *my* dad would break out of gaol to see me, do you?' Joy asked sneeringly. But she felt better once she had admitted it: that she was jealous of Ronnie Starr; she was jealous of that poor, scared, unhappy boy, because his father had wanted, more than anything, despite everything, to spend time with him.

'Yes, he probably would,' said Holly decidedly, and Joy knew then and there that she would not phone the police about the convict in the barn. She was not that petty or vindictive.

'We'll have to do something about Mel,' she said, purposefully changing the subject. 'He's taken a big dislike to Ronnie Starr, and besides, he'd tell anybody anything. They do at that age.'

'You leave it to F.C.,' said Holly with one of her broad, elfin grins, 'He'll have Mel standing guard at the barn door before he knows: guarding the secret with his life. He can do that with little kids. It's something about Grandpa.'

'I s'pect it's hereditary,' said Joy narrowing her eyes at the elf.

As they went towards the barn, a bright prism of condensed light came speeding up the long drive from the main road, resolving itself into the shape and roar of a coach. Big purple clouds were building up over Cold Pike, compressing the heat, turning it back on to the house and garden in stifling layers. The elderly men and women aboard the coach pointed knobbly fingers at the massing thunderclouds, and mouthed the word RAIN like two dozen soothsayers. The driver saw the girls, and waved as he pulled into the car park, displacing large swirls of gravel, following a well-worn circle.

It was the same coach-driver the Shepherds had seen as they first trudged up the drive: close-cropped hair, puce with heat, and (by the look of him) savagely gregarious.

'That's Charlie All-Right,' said Holly out of the corner of her mouth. 'Such promise written on his face, and then all he ever says is . . . '

'All right?' called Charlie the coach-driver. As the heat-tormented British Legionnaires climbed painfully down from the coach, Holly and Joy slipped inside the barn.

'Mr Starr! Mr Starr?' Holly called softly as the chickens gathered around her feet. The heat in the tin barn was appalling.

His accountant's face appeared over a straw bale, the gooseberry-green eyes glaucous with worry. Holly nudged Joy. 'You decided,' she said. 'You tell him.'

Joy blushed. 'Oh, it's . . . er . . . I er . . . It's all right for you to stay, that's all,' she called up shyly.

'That's good. That's fine. Thank you. That's first rate. Excellent,' said Mr Starr. Very little of the anxiety abated from his face, but then why should it? His overall predicament was very little helped by a few hours' sanctuary. But he dredged up a smile of expressible gratitude. 'Just a couple of days. To get straight inside myself. Put things right with Ronnie here. I never had time to put things right. Before.'

Ronnie Starr jumped up into view, throwing handfuls of straw in the air and grinning madly. For him, their success in eluding the police had turned grim misfortune into an adventure, a game. Suddenly he was having the time of his life.

We'll be gone tomorrow, thought Joy. Never see how it turns out in the end. And she realized that she, too, was watching events as if on TV. Sometimes it felt as if she would always be a watcher, a spectator, an on-looker, at one remove.

'I'll bring you some games over, shall I?' Holly was saying. 'And crackers, and some sweets. Try to keep hidden: we've got a houseful this afternoon.'

Suddenly the barn door slid open, and a blade of sunlight fell like a guillotine across Joy who froze in guilty terror. Adrenalin rushed in at her stomach.

'All right?' said the silhouette in the doorway.

Joy could not speak.

'Fine thanks, Charlie,' said Holly. 'Yourself?'

But the taciturn Charlie had already turned and slid the barn door closed again.

Holly began to giggle; Joy joined in, and their laughing set the hens fussing and fleeing outside and under the cars. That made them giggle even more, until they were leaning on each other, breathless.

But when they emerged from the barn, Charlie All-Right had made an unprecedented break in his usual rigid routine and was sitting directly opposite them, a good way off, on the garden bench.

'Not going down to the pub, Charlie?' asked Holly.

Charlie sucked air in sharply through his teeth. 'Not with the police parked up outside your gate. They'll be tandem breathalysing, that's what. So I'm staying put right here, all right?'

'The police are parked outside the gate?'

'Right! Police all over 'tween here and the motorway. Never seen the like.'

The girls glanced at each other, fellow conspirators. 'You'd best come in and have some lunch, then, Charlie,' said Holly. 'You can't sit there just staring at the barn all afternoon.'

The man jumped up willingly. 'Righto!'

The ice-cream in Mel's cone melted almost as quickly as his hopes of Christmas. He felt the same kind of desperation as he chased the drips with his tongue.

When his sister and the elf disappeared into the cupboard under the stairs, he wanted to go in with them but they said no, said he must take his ice-cream out into the garden. Of course. There were stockings hanging up in the cupboard under the stairs. He even thought he heard F.C.'s voice in there: naturally Mel was barred from such a place. Mel, for some heinous unspoken crime he was unaware of, must never be allowed into such places.

He went straight back to the willow tree, but there was no one there, not even the Starrs. His fingers, gummy with ice-cream, began to stick together as if he were turning into a frog, web-footed. He went to look at the donkey, but it was lying on its side in the paddock, pole-axed by the heat, and would not get up. He went to see the chickens in the barn, but they had wandered outside and were sleeping under the parked cars. Even shouting did not rouse them.

He went to look for their eggs. The tin barn was like a furnace, its rivets clicking, its rural smell fusing into an incandescent sweetness. There was a new, peculiar atmosphere to the place—as if someone was already in there. Watching. He shouted out, but when no one answered decided to explore. There was a ladder leading up to the loft now, which had not been there when he and F.C. had commandeered the lawn-mower. Since the loft seemed a promising place for eggs, he started to climb.

All of a sudden, an egg struck him on the shoulder. The shell broke. The yellow globule inside clung to his shirt, clear jelly crawling down into his breast pocket. Then someone unseen took hold of the top of the ladder and pushed it away from the loft, so that Mel was tipped over backwards. He was no more than two or three rungs off the floor, but the ladder was heavy and he thought it was going to fall on top of him. Instead, its top end struck the barn wall. He was jarred loose, and landed in a heap on the floor.

Mel pelted out of the barn as far and as fast as his frightened legs would carry him: their bones felt hollow. The ice-cream mounted into his throat, and he was sick against the house wall.

'Aye up!' said a familiar voice. 'Something you ate?'

'Oh! It's you!'

F.C leaning out of his ground-floor bedroom window, wonderfully on cue, marvellously cheering, startlingly frail.

He too seemed to have patches of ice cream whiteness on his cheeks and jowls.

'The barn's haunted!' exclaimed Mel.

'Is that a fact! Well, don't you go anywhere near it then, eh?'

F.C. stepped aside as Mel, uninvited, climbed in at the window. The child did not think to ask permission—in fact he was faintly surprised that F.C. did not help him more, given the closeness of their friendship. By the time Mel had negotiated the sill, the old man was sitting on his bed, hunched forwards, uncomfortable-looking and dishevelled.

'Is this where you live?' said Mel, instantly distracted.

'Aye. Around these parts.'

'I forgot to tell you. I want a pet. Anything alive. Anything. Really! Joy won't let me go in the cupboard with her. The ghost threw an egg at me! Dad says I can't have one, but I can, can't I? An animal? Some kind of animal? On TV I saw this cartoon and you—'

'Would you stack some pillows up for me, there's a good boy,' said F.C.

Mel made a clumsy pile in the middle of the bed, thinking they were the makings of a game. But F.C. only leaned back into them. Two pillows slid off on to the floor; F.C. made no move to pick them up. He remained listing ungainly against the rest, like a turtle unable to right itself. 'I'll buck up in a tick,' he said.

Mel's fright returned. 'Wha's the matter?'

'Oh, just something I ate, like you, like as not.' But there was a crumpled paper in the old man's hand: somebody's wish. He did not seem able or willing to put it down. His thin, big-knuckled fingers kept stroking the surface of the page, as if the message were punched out in Braille. There was not much to the wish, Mel could see that.

'Wha's up?' said Mel again.

F.C. gave an imperceptible wave of his hand, lifting it off his chest as if it weighed a great deal . . . 'It's the Starrs, Mel. They're in a spot of trouble. So we have to help them out, don't we? Only neighbourly.'

'Oh,' said Mel, peeved. 'All right.'

'Thought I might take them out for a spin later. Take them somewhere . . . when I've bucked up a mite.' He began to pant, taking little shallow breaths which hollowed out the grooves in his thin neck. 'Sometimes I get just a tad sad about the state folks get themselves in. It's t'otherside of enjoying folk. Nothing for you to worry your head about, though. *Hakuna matata*, we say, don't we, lad?'

But Mel said no such thing. Capable of bottomless greed, self-seeking, jealousy and wilfulness, Mel owned all the other qualities of a four year old: great tide rips of sympathy, empathy, generosity. Huge unformed waves of caring welled up in his little frame now. He wanted to fling his arms around Santa Claus and raise him up bodily out of his sorrows.

'I could ask the Angel to make you better!' he burst out, and the old man was touched.

'That's the ticket, lad,' he said vaguely. 'You ask the angels to help us out of this little . . . pickle we're in.' The pills for his angina were starting to take effect. The pain in his chest was subsiding, leaving only a bruising around his soul made by the manifold worries of the day.

7
Good Health

With the arrival of the British Legion, Mr Angel resolved to leave at once. He could not stomach Forever Xmas. Though unable to catch them out in any heinous contravention of the health and safety regulations, he hated the whole absurd idea of the place. A hotel given over to Christmas? Even in its right and proper place, Mr Angel hated Christmas, its saccharine sentimentality, its wilful harping back to older, dirtier times. Children (though he saw himself as daily preserving their lives from botulism, staphylococcus, listeria, salmonella and so forth) were not to his taste, being disorganized and unpredictable. Now this influx of elderly people, deliberately subjecting themselves to Christmas in August, made him tremble with loathing. They would inevitably start singing, playing bingo, engaging in old-time dancing. The heat was making him ill, and—most galling of all—he had failed to keep secret his identity from the staff.

It always gave Mr Angel pleasure: that moment when he threw wide the kitchen door and declared himself: 'I am an accredited inspector for the Environmental Health Department!'; the flurry of guilty panic as he flashed his identification card like an agent of the FBI. Mr Angel prided himself on his ability to blend in with his surroundings in any kind of catering outlet. But here, even that small pleasure had been denied him by the police hunt. He had had to unmask and come clean—show his identity to the sergeant, explain the purpose of his visit. When at last he had made his surprise foray into the kitchen of Forever Xmas, the proprietor—he of the

1940s haircut and hangdog expression—had simply looked up and said, 'We were expecting you.'

Everything had been spotless, of course. Give these people the smallest inch and they escaped retribution with a few wipes of a disinfectant cloth. It was a great shame. Perhaps he should leave now and cut his losses. He could barely face another meal of turkey, and he had only been on the premises for a day. Yes, Mr Angel decided, he would go now.

He refolded his napkin and gathered up his papers. Somehow he had managed to pick up a pink circular from his room entitled *A Message for Snata*. He made to screw it up and then, in a moment of spleen, scribbled ferociously across the space left blank for wishes, '*I wish I had the power to close down this place.*'

Pinching the paper into a small pink pellet, he pitched it at the Christmas tree.

'You don't have to give me an animal.'

Angel looked round. Mel's head came only to a level with the table top, his upturned face the same size and roundness of a sideplate. He was only just visible. 'Are you talking to me?'

'What I really wanted was an animal. More than anything.'

'Thank you for sharing that with me,' said Angel nasally.

'I was going to say it. But then Ronnie came. And we have to go tomorrow.'

This was what Angel chiefly hated about children, the random outpouring of disconnected thoughts—like a Virginia Woolf novel on legs, a one-man play by Becket in far too many acts.

'You're Health, though, aren't you?' said the boy. Angel was startled by this sudden ray of clarity. 'You're in charge of Health, aren't you?'

'I am, yes. I do, in a manner of speaking . . . '

'Only he's sick. He says it's something he ate, but he's all grey and badly, and I don't mind really, if he needs my wish. Dad doesn't like animals, anyway. He'd never've let me keep one. So I'll change my wish. You being Health . . .'

The words bombarded Angel like a shower of coins, and here and there he saw a glint which pleased him. Someone was sick from food poisoning. Someone in this house. A stab of superstitious foolishness made him think of his own pink wish lying screwed up under the Christmas tree.

Angel glanced quickly at the long buffet table, the three slab-like birds arrayed like sacrifices on an altar. A long queue was starting to form of spruce old ladies with white hair and cotton sleeveless blouses, each cradling her handbag. They talked, one over the other, as if at any moment the world's supply of words might dry up, and their excitable chorus fuelled Angel's aggression even more. It would be a risk, but one he had to take.

Jumping to his feet, he crossed the dining room. Flouting the queue, he went directly to the turkey, the central turkey. It lay on its back, like a dog seeking affection. Snatching up the carvers, he impaled the carcass, while his knife-hand struck the mortal blow. Snow-white flesh sagged away from the breastbone—white meat and lightly pink meat and, at the very innermost recesses of the carcass—*blood!*

Mel stared. Standing close behind the Angel of Health, he watched the seraphim perform this strange, primordial rite, some fearful violent act of sacrificial magic, slashing a turkey to the bone. Was this what it took to grant his wish? To restore F.C. to health?

Triumphant, Angel brandished the carving knife aloft and looked around for either of the proprietors. But in the absence of Ivy and Colin Partridge, the only member of the household he could see was the elf-girl, collecting soup dishes.

'Got you!' he said, pointing the knife accusingly at her head.

Holly burst into tears, and ran out of the room.

Folding the front of the paper tablecloth up over the undercooked turkeys, without a word of explanation to the queue, he went to his room to fetch the requisite notices from his briefcase—notices which would cordon off the condemned food like an unexploded bomb.

'What did you say to him, you little wretch?'

Joy caught her little brother by the biceps and spun him round to face her. Her face was as disarranged as a picture by Picasso; to Mel the eyes and nose and brows and mouth seemed to be in the wrong places. *'You told him about Ronnie, didn't you? You told him about the Starrs! Now we'll all go to prison, and it'll all be your fault!'*

Mel stared back at her, his face a blank. He was Alice through the Looking Glass; everything was in reverse. What ought to be happiness was misery; the angels were fierce, the elves were cruel, and his hardest attempts to do right only got him into deeper and deeper trouble. 'I just changed my wish, 'cos Father Christmas—'

'He'll be taken too, you know! You needn't think you'll get him to yourself that way! We'll all get arrested!' She hissed it into his face, bending down for the sole purpose of spitting her words into his wide-open eyes. Mel's heart clattered about inside him like a calf in a crate. He thought he would die of fright. In all his life he had never seen his sister like this. And for what? Because he had wanted to wish Father Christmas back to health?

Joy did not know what she had seen—only her little brother standing beside Angel's table, babbling, bright-eyed and flushed, and Angel's triumphant, vindictive reaction. She did not see the turkey carcass drip its sinful blood, only the symbolic blow of a sadistic man who has just found evidence enough to damn his enemies. Combined with the knowledge that the police were parked at the end of the drive, it was enough to convince Joy that a terrible retribution was on its way, and that her little brother had personally brought it about.

She also saw the room-key on Angel's table. She did not know why she picked it up—only that Angel would be the worse off for it. Then she went looking for the elf, but collided with Colin Partridge in the doorway.

'Joy, come back here and sit down!' called her father, while her mother mopped up Mel's tears and tried to make sense of what had happened.

'Just got to go and . . . ' said Joy, in vague, conversational tones. The noise from the British Legion was huge. There was no chance her father would hear her excuse, so why invent one?

'Now, help yourselves, help yourselves,' Colin Partridge urged the diners, swiftly folding down the paper table cloth which (he believed) the draught from the open window must have lifted over the turkeys. 'And then, before our VIP visitor arrives, what about a nice game of bingo?'

'Oh good grief . . . ' Joy saw her father say; she could almost hear the grinding of his teeth. Mrs Shepherd covered his arm with her hand, that pained, headachy look on her face and her other hand on the wine bottle, pouring him another glass.

Joy looked everywhere for Holly. She found Mrs Partridge in the kitchen, crying, found Charlie the coach-driver in the yard—'All right?'—and lastly F.C. just emerging from his room wearing his full Santa Claus costume: the beard, hat, and red woollen jacket. He was feeling much better after his nap.

'It's all up!' said Joy histrionically, grabbing him by the fur of his cuff. 'Mel's told Angel, I'm sure he has! The police are parked by the gate! It's all coming apart!'

His face was inexpressive behind the beard, but he fumbled in his pocket for a set of car keys he had not owned in years. She looked into his milky blue eyes and thought, just fleetingly, 'Why am I telling this loopy old man? What can he do?'

But then the eyes subtly changed—cleared—and she felt him lift the responsibility off her shoulders, as surely as if he had crammed it into his Santa sack.

'Happen you'd best tell the Starrs. Change of plan. Time to shift ground. Where's Colin?'

'Fetching dinner to the invalids who can't queue.'

'Well, you run and ask him for the car keys, pet.'

But Colin Partridge did not have the car keys. Between filling plates and taking requests, he explained that the keys were in his wife's handbag in the kitchen. Filled with unease, he began to drop sprouts off the serving spoon and chase them along the paper tablecloth.

Joy found F.C. standing in the open doorway, his feet walking on the spot, like an automaton Santa.

'No keys—unless I ask Mrs Partridge for them.'

'I don't think that would do, lass.'

'There's the coach!' said Joy. 'We could take the coach! They'd think it was Charlie going down the pub!'

'Fair enough. I'll tell the Starrs.'

He entered the heat of the garden, like a red beetle stepping into a lump of amber, all his movements slowed by the sheer density of the sunshine, his outline broken up by the flaring glare. And Joy, with unformed thoughts of begging Angel to be merciful, climbed the stairs to his room, the key clutched between her fingers like a knuckle-duster.

Angel had not noticed the lack of his key, having left his bedroom door open for cleaning. She could see him pulling papers out of his briefcase and tossing them on the bed. He had half-packed his suitcase, too: green lovat trousers, green lovat pullover, memo machine, green ties. And on a rash whim—without thought of consequences or even why she was doing it—Joy pulled the door shut and locked it with Angel's own key.

From inside came a startled grunt, a tentative call—'who's there?'—but nobody was. Joy was already flying down the stairs, her thoughts spinning like the figures in a fairground centrifuge, pinned haphazardly to the wall of her brain, upside-down and hugger-mugger.

She ran straight out of the door and over to the coach, jumping aboard it behind Ronnie Starr, who started like a jack rabbit at the thud of her feet. All the boy's cocky brashness was gone now, and his hands were knotted anxiously into the half-belt of his father's jacket.

'Reckon I'll take you to our place. Our family place,' F.C. was saying, in a bright, calm voice. 'Beach chalet at Workington. Used to go there every summer.' His voice was so soothing, so jolly.

Like our caravan in Linstock, thought Joy, except that F.C. managed to make the chalet sound fun. He made everything sound fun. And safe.

'Now if you'll just crouch down between the seats and keep right out of sight, we shouldn't have a mite trouble,' he said. Made it sound easy.

Charlie the coach-driver, asleep on the garden bench, started up at the sound of the big diesel engine turning over. He swung his legs off the bench and strolled up; Joy watched him coming in the wing mirror. Crouched up on her knees on the courier's seat, she punched the upholstery. '*Well? Why don't you go?*' she shrieked. '*Just drive off! He'll be here in a second!*'

61

'Take the man's coach without asking?' said F.C. peaceably. 'He *would* be vexed.'

Charlie stuck his head in at the open coach door. 'All right?' he said, looking round the empty bus.

'Just telling the girlie how I used to drive one of these. Do a spin, can I? Good lad.'

'Ah well, I . . . ' While Charlie struggled with massive abstract concepts such as insurance and liability, failing to find the words, F.C. put the coach into gear with a shudder and a cough, and moved serenely away over the crunching gravel.

8
Sleighride

'You really shouldn't be on here, lass, now I think it,' said F.C. 'Best drop you off at the end of the lane.' He took off his beard and rested it on the dashboard. He pulled off his hat and waved it at the police parked in the car beside the gate. 'All right?' he mouthed at them through the glass. (Perhaps there was something about the isolation of that high, glass driving booth that rendered down communication, like bacon fat.)

The officers made no move to stop the coach and search it. Perhaps even in them lurked the deep-seated conviction that the-man-in-the-red-suit had to be trustworthy.

Aboard the coach, there was a feeling of pressure suddenly released. Escaping from Forever Xmas was like escaping from a single day into an expanse of time 364 times bigger. Starr and Ronnie came out from hiding, and swayed forwards down the bus wreathed in smiles, triumphant. F.C. slipped his arms out of his coat as he drove, displaying cheery red braces. The coach flashed down narrow lanes, between dry stone walls and plaited hazel hedges, between fountains of yellow gorse and fellsides as faceted as ancient Roman mosaics in purple and mauve. Now and then, the screen turned into an opaque sheet of pure sunlight, and F.C. stabbed at the brakes, making the others reel and roar with laughter.

'I can't thank you enough,' began Starr in his clipped, accountant's voice, precise as a four-column ledger.

F.C. held up a hand. 'Don't mention it. It's what we do. What we're here for. Holly said that.' F.C. was in anarchic mood, and it suited him. He too had escaped on to a larger plain. Here was wish-fulfilment on the grand scale, more to his taste than doling out bottles of Sanatogen and lottery dice as an after-dinner diversion. He rooted about among Charlie's cassette tapes, and rammed home the *Readers Digest* All-Time Classic Greats, so that 'Night on a Bare Mountain' blared out down the bus. He had time for men like Starr who would risk future disaster in return for present laughter.

'F.C.—' Joy began.

'Felix Cox,' he declared, bursting into his own identity having peeled off his other one.

Joy thought about this. 'So that's where the X came from.'

'What?'

'The X in "Forever Xmas". All the X's in your name.'

F.C. accelerated out of a bend. The cloud-filled expanse of Bassenthwaite came into sight, a flotilla of red-sailed yachts tacking across the surface, like kites in a blue sky. Beyond it, a fire was burning somewhere in Skiddaw Forest. 'Never liked that X,' he growled. 'To my mind, it's a cop-out and a blasphemy. I said to them: is it the Jewish trade or the Muslims you're scared of losing? But Ivy thought we might get taken for Evangelicals. So they went for Xmas. X marks the spot. Brand X—the one what doesn't wash whiter.'

Joy stood with her knees braced against the seats, feeling the bobble of the wheels over an uneven road surface, feeling like a charioteer hurtling towards some battle deadly and marvellous. 'I locked Mr Angel in his bedroom,' she confessed, exhilarated that she felt no guilt. 'That should slow him up!'

'Grand!' exclaimed F.C. and blared the horn at a flock of crows pecking something in the road.

The scenery of the Lakes gave way to an oddly grim, industrial hinterland, and then the sea, steely and flat after the crashing wavescape of the fells. Little rows of solid, stolid houses turned side-on to the ocean, like trains coming into the buffers of a large station. Little seaside shops extruded inflatable beach toys, like faces blowing bubble gum. F.C. drove the coach into the new marina car park, leaning over the wheel to turn it and the coach with a gesture of panache.

Ronnie Starr sat gripping his father's hand, gazing at the sea as though it had come at his bidding, at a whistle. After the frightening confines of the hotel, the boy's soul leapt forwards out of his eyes, running down the pebble beach ahead of him.

The beach had been busy—the heatwave had kept it full for weeks—but now rain was spitting out of a clear blue sky—turn of the tide?—and deck-chairs stood about gawky and gangling, their striped canvas blowing inside out. Perhaps Ronnie thought that he and his father could run between them and out across that dense oily sea to a freedom as big as the world.

'Our chalet is 71,' F.C. was saying to the boy's father. 'It's a fair walk—mile or more down that way, but the coach could get itself noticed any place but here. Sort of green-and-reddish, you're looking for. Have to force the padlock, but there's a little primus stove in there, and some bits and bobs. Bucket and spade, that manner of thing. You'll need a bit of brass for groceries. You got a bit of brass?'

'I've got brass,' said Starr flattening the 'a', despite his southernness. 'Two days. I'll give Ronnie two days, then I'll turn myself in, I swear.' But the vocabulary of criminality did not sit right on Mr Starr; it was as if he had picked it up from a TV programme he did not much enjoy. 'Two days, I swear.'

'Some days can be bigger than others,' said F.C. nodding his bony head. 'Two'll be grand.'

Starr shook his hand—would have liked to spend more time finding the right words, but Ronnie was tugging on his other hand, trying to get him off the bus, eager to get started on the fun, ruthless in wanting his father to himself. F.C. called out a goodbye, but Ronnie had no words to spare for anyone but his father. He turned his back and blocked the other out of mind with looking at the sea.

'I suppose we'd better get back,' said Joy, wistfully, as the Starrs pottered out of sight.

'Ooo, no hurry, no hurry,' said F.C. He sounded sleepy, in need of a nap.

'Can I go down and paddle, then?' said Joy. 'Seeing as we're here. . . . You could come, too.'

But F.C. sent her down to the water's edge by herself, with money to bring them both back an ice-cream. It was delectable, standing thigh-deep in the sea; it felt icy against her hot legs, and her wet trousers would keep her cool on the way back. The pupils of her eyes shut down so tight against the brightness that she could see only a blackened shadowplay of movement and feel the muddy sand groove and slip away from under her feet.

There was not a sign of the Starrs any longer. It was as if they had never been—mirages raised up by the heat. Only a lingering feeling remained to her of having stepped outside everyday bounds, having broken out of childhood into a bigger, scarier world where right and wrong were not so hard and fast. Even they had melted into one another in this endless heatwave.

Suddenly a tremendous crash of thunder set the sea shivering in a thousand catspaws. She felt the sound thud against her breastbone, and it left its echo singing in her ears. She picked her way laboriously up the beach, shoes dangling from her fingers, hair catching in the corners of her mouth. By the time she got to the ice-cream booth, its shutters were up, but the man gave her two Callipos instead of soft-cones. He had turned the machine off, he said.

F.C. was sitting at the wheel of the coach just as before, except that his face looked greyer. Everything—skin, beard, hair—seemed greyer, and when she held out the icy cardboard tube to him he did not take it, did not turn to look at her or even blink an eye.

She knew he was dead, even though she had never seen a person dead before, and the sight did not excite in her thoughts of rescue, first aid, panic or screaming. Rescues were F.C.'s prerogative. She simply stood on the running board and faced the same way as he, while big white drops of rain hit and streaked the wide glass screen. Inside her pocket, her fingers closed around a piece of folded paper: the *Letter to Snata* she had declined to fill in. She pulled it out now. It was blank. As blank as the sensation in her chest.

Joy thought through the implications. She did not want F.C. slighted by the police, reduced in status to a criminal nuisance who had briefly thwarted them. Neither did she want to destroy his achievement, his gift to the Starrs, the parcel of Christmas he had given them. So she took a chewed biro from the map-holder on the facia and wrote a few words.

To go to the seaside.

When she called the police, as she supposed she must, they would ask what Felix Cox had been doing driving a coach to Workington wearing a Santa Claus costume.

'I made a wish,' she would say. 'He granted it. That's what Felix did,' she would say, 'he granted wishes.'

What better could you say of anyone?

F.C. continued to look out to sea, still and resolute and undefeated. Only his colour was diminished, pallor settling over him like a fall of snow.

9

Angel on the Tree

'Where has he gone? Where've they gone?' Mel ran up and down the hall, making the angel chimes tremble, and pulling his mother's skirt askew.

Unable to quiet Mel's crying, Mrs Shepherd had gone in search of her daughter to find out just what could have caused her to attack her little brother. She was just in time to see the coach drive off down the track with Charlie hopping irresolutely after it. It was Charlie who told her that F.C. and Joy were aboard.

Then Mel came snivelling into the hall. 'Where's he gone? Where's Father Christmas gone?' He did not see the coach leaving.

'He's just taken Joy on a nice . . . ' But his mother could not finish. She was too worried and put out to bother putting a pleasant gloss on events which were slipping out of her control.

'Where's he taken her? S'not fair! S'not fair!' Mel was beside himself with uncomprehending jealousy, once more bereft of Father Christmas.

'They'll be back shortly, dear,' said his mother soothingly, but her own alarm transmitted itself to the child. Where *had* they gone? Mel asked everyone.

'Santa's gone to his . . . er . . . to his holiday place,' said Colin Partridge, reading the note scribbled on the message pad by the hall phone. He tore the note off, too, and screwed it into a tiny ball which he lost in a trouser pocket. *Taken Ronnie etc. to our chalet*, the note said.

'His special place? The place he told me about?' said Mel.

68

'I expect so, yes,' said the hotelier, grateful to be believed.

'But he said he'd take me, not her! He said he'd take me!' Mel dragged so hard on his mother's skirt that the pleats all turned round to one side. He was demanding arbitration, but the referees in this game seemed to have lost all control of play. His mother was angry and upset—'No one mentioned an outing. I wasn't asked my permission . . . ' she said, and Colin Partridge extricated himself hastily and went to check something about the barn—which was an odd thing to do in the supposed middle of a bingo game.

The British Legionnaires were getting restive. Rumours were spreading (thanks to Mel's noise) that Father Christmas would not turn up with their presents either. Ivy Partridge had steered them towards Black Forest gateaux, to mollify them, but she was starting to feel excluded herself from some secret the rest of her family knew about. She was heard to say, as she wheeled the video trolley into the parlour and set the Royal Address playing, 'Thank God for the Queen.'

Holly was kept busier than ever. She took over calling bingo for her father, pulled crackers with the guests, collected in their wishes, microwaved Christmas puddings, and cleared tables.

Meanwhile, Mel racked his brains, wondering where Santa's special place might be, so that he could get there and share in his sister's undeserved happiness. Might it be that F.C. was simply showing her the barn, the chickens, the lawnmower? It was worth a look. So Mel ran to the barn and searched, and his mother let him go, not knowing what else would pacify him.

He succeeded, this time, in resting the ladder back up against the hayloft, and was so full of aggression and resentment that he even dared climb it, shouting abuse at the invisible enemy who had previously spilled him off the rungs. But there was no enemy at the top of the ladder—only

69

evidence enough to show that Mr Starr and Ronnie had been there. Always them. Always getting to a place before him. He had not really expected the 'special place' to be there. They had gone, he was sure, up the mountains to the place his F.C. had spoken of: with eagles and ravens. He pictured the kind of birds he had seen in church holding up the lectern. Only now they were holding up a ledge, a plateau, a region of cloud and majesty and rapture. Like a fat little hen, he sat and brooded in the hayloft until he fell asleep, thumb in mouth, curled up among Ronnie's discarded chocolate wrappers. His mother, when she came looking for him, found him there and left him, because he looked so charming and peaceful.

When Mel woke an hour later, he went out into the yard, to the blare of the chickens and the docile indifference of the donkey. Now he taxed his brain with wondering: would they ever return, F.C. and his sister? Assuming, from Joy's words, that she and F.C. were on the run from the police, when, if ever, would they leave Santa's 'special place' and come home?

He even managed to get on to the donkey's back—it was astonishingly hard and bony, but his mother saw him from the window and beckoned for him to come in, pointing at the blackening sky. He nodded in reply. After she looked away, however, a sudden clap of thunder scared the donkey into a trot, and Mel slid off on to the ground. But his mother did not see that, so did not come to pick him up.

It seemed to Mel then as if all his unshed tears were suddenly falling on the ground around him: big dark explosions of wet kicking up the dust. Abruptly, the rain emptied itself over his head like the contents of a bucket. Mouth open, lips as rigid and silent as the trumpet of a daffodil, he sat and felt the rain course through his hair, his eyebrows, his lashes.

Cold Pike disappeared; a grey, opaque curtain drawn across it, billowing in dirty folds out over house and lake and the Wrinkles. Twisters of rainwater chased each other up and down the car park, as if looking for the absent coach, enlivening the oil streaks into trickles of rainbow. The rain struck amazingly cold at first, then warmed inside Mel's clothing, worming down inside pants and socks. The storm, moving in from the west and the sea, grew louder as it arrived overhead, the thunderclaps more frequent, more synchronized with the flashes of lightning. It was just as if the gods were throwing thunderbolts now at his miserable head, enraged by that unwitting crime of his (whatever it was) and bent on purging the valley of Mel the Sinner.

He ran back to the barn, but every flash of lightning illuminated the seams and holes in the corrugated metal. He also knew enough to recall how metal drew lightning, and envisaged the walls as live and lethal as an electric ray swimming over his head. So he quit the barn and ran for the willow tree.

Its umbrella of leaves was as leaky as a sieve; it allowed the rain to pour down unabated on his head, while the weepers lashed in an angry hula-hula, licked him, and left their narrow green tongues stuck to his legs. Besides, he remembered now that lightning strikes trees, too, and that only fools shelter under trees in a storm. He quit the willow tree for the house.

And there, at the end of the hotel building, where a conserved elm tree had prevented the building of a fire escape, where Room 7 looked out over the Pike, where a blocked gutter fumed with water running off the roof, Mel saw him—saw Mr Angel—saw Angel on the tree.

Locked into his room, unable to attract attention (thanks to the sound-proof fire-doors and the noise of the British Legion), Mr Angel had gradually grown desperate and resorted to self-help. Opening the big sash window, he had climbed out on to the limbs of the big elm. The branches were broad and level: traversing had been easy, as far as the trunk. But then his courage had failed him. Unlike Holly, he had not been shinning up and down this tree all his life; it would not render up its secrets to him, a stranger. The distance between the tiers of branches suddenly seemed much too great for him simply to lower himself down. And when the storm broke, and the branches became instantly wet and slippery, he found he dared not risk even climbing back to the window.

By the time Mel Shepherd appeared below him, as small and wet as a fractured hydrant, Mr Angel had been in the tree more than an hour, hoping for rescue. To ease his cramped legs, he had just now stood up on the branch again, sodden leather shoes discarded, arms outstretched to aid balance. Mel only saw him because a burst of lightning, like the sky short-circuiting, back-lit the tree and revealed his figure, cruciform, on the rain-silvered tree. His tightly curled hair was illuminated, his face ash-white in the stark brilliance. Leaves had stuck themselves to every conceivable part of his suit: a seraphim caught in the unrecorded act of ascent or descent.

Taking to wing or coming in to land.

If Mel had ever doubted the divine nature of Mr Angel, all doubts were erased now. For how else did Angel come to be there, at the top of a tall tree, in a rainstorm, unless he had either flown up or flown back to roost there after an excursion through the ether.

'Are you going too?' asked Mel.

'Too bloody right. The moment I get d—'

'To the same place?' Mel wanted to know. 'To Santa's secret place? Up there?'

'Don't stand there gawping, you stupid child. Go and get your father. Get the proprietors. Get anyone.'

'Can I come?' said Mel. 'Will you take me with you?'

A trident of lightning quivering directly over his head made Angel duck and cower down. He wanted to hurl abuse at this obstructive, babbling, unhelpful, moronic little runt . . . but dared not antagonize him. 'Please. Be a good boy now,' he said in unaccustomed tones of cajoling gentleness. 'You just go and get your dad, and there's twenty pence in it for you.'

'In what?'

'Fifty. Just do it.'

'Show me your wings first. I want to see your wings.' With his face turned flat up to the sky, the rain kept falling into Mel's eyes, even though he squeezed them thin as slits.

'Just go and get bloody someone, will you?' roared the seraphim out of the tree, and Mel turned and ran, his flat feet splashing up water off ground too hard to drink the rain.

He ran in at the kitchen door, but Mrs Partridge was in the walk-in larder and only heard the door bang. He ran across the hall and into the parlour where nineteen elderly men and women were marvelling at the heaviness of the downpour.

'One for the record books, I reckon,' said a heather-coloured lady in a heather-coloured Gor-Ray skirt.

'The Angel's on the tree!' Mel told her.

She bent down her head to him, wide-eyed. 'Yes, that's right, dear. It is, isn't it? I saw it.' She drew her friends attention to the little boy, smiling indulgently.

'*The Angel's on the tree!*' Mel told her friend with as much urgency as he could lend it, clenching his fists, his face, his body. He could not understand why they did not comprehend the wonder of what he was telling them. Surely these people did not see real angels every day of the week?

'Ahhhh,' said the woman and smiled back at her friend. 'In't that luvly, Laura?'

They passed him round from one purple-veined hand to the next, some touching his hair. Some were concerned that he was so wet. Most just delighted in his innocent wonder at discovering the angel on the Christmas tree.

'Shall we go and look at it together, sweetheart?' said a grandmotherly lady with yellow-tinted glasses. But she would not, despite all his demands and pleas, follow him further than the dining room and the foot of the tall, glittering spruce in its red plastic pot.

In the end Mel had to return to the garden, for fear the seraphim grew impatient and left for Heaven without him, soaring into the crazy-paving sky, hop-scotching between cracks of lightning. 'I told them,' said Mel to the angel in the tree.

'And?'

'They didn't understand.'

Angel swore and slapped his hand against the tree trunk.

'You've got to go up there. You've got to tell him. I want Joy back. Joy says the police'll come and arrest him. But I won't let them. Daddy won't let them. Mummy won't let them. I don't know what I done. But you got to tell him: I didn't mean it! I didn't do nothing hardly. You are going there, aren't you. Aren't you?'

'God Almighty!'

'Oh, not there! Not first, anyway! First you got to go up to F.C.! To his secret place! Up the mountain! Tell him I didn't mean it! Tell him I'm sorry. Tell him to come back! And Joy! Tell them I didn't do nothing hardly!'

Exasperated, seething, soaked, and scared, Mr Angel perceived no shred of coherent thought in Mel's outpourings. They welled out of the child's mouth along with rainwater and tears—a stream of nonsense it was beneath the man's dignity to puzzle over.

'You've got to make it all right! You've got to! It's your

74

job! All right, you just tell God. Tell Him to help! Tell Him I'm sorry! Tell Him F.C. didn't do anything wrong ever! It was only me!'

At that moment, a police car, needing its headlights to see through the stygian rain, came racing up the drive. The rutted surface of the track made the car pitch, so that the beams raked the hotel like searchlights and illuminated the pelting rain.

To Mel it was Nemesis approaching, the unjust punishment Joy had promised would fall on her, on Holly, on F.C., on everyone. The police were coming to arrest everyone he loved, because of something—if only he knew what—something Mel had done.

'Tell God to help us!' he demanded of the seraphim in the tree. Then he turned and ran towards the base of Third Wrinkle.

To Jack Shepherd it was like seeing his daughter after a great time apart from her; she seemed so changed. All around them the British Legion were fussing and fuming, discovering one by one that their coach was not outside, that it would be some time in coming, that they might have to stay overnight. Colin Partridge was trying to appease them with Black Forest gateaux and free use of the phone. Someone said that the old man was dead, had been found dead.

And yet all Jack Shepherd could see was that plate-white oval of his daughter's face, so blank, so sad, so . . . grown up.

'Is it true? Was there a crash? Was the old man killed?' he asked the police who had brought Joy home. The red Santa jacket hung folded over the girl's clasped hands.

The police told him no, it had been nothing like that. Just a heart attack. At the seaside in Workington. No one hurt. No one else hurt. Jack put his arm round Joy's shoulders, turned her face against his chest in case she wanted to cry. But she remained dry-eyed, inexpressive, and as soon as she could, moved away, her thoughts still somewhere else, in a different town, with someone other than him.

'You liked him, did you? Old Mr Partridge?' said her father tentatively.

'Cox. His name was Cox. He's Ivy's father.'

'Fun, though, was he? I know Mel thinks . . . thought the world of him. I didn't realize you . . . '

'He was different. He was out of it. He did wishes,' said Joy. 'You wouldn't understand.'

And suddenly he knew how his son Mel had felt to be excluded from Christmas, to be denied access to somewhere important. The death of his own childhood had passed unnoticed, unregretted, years ago. But now he was confronted with losing something much worse: the vicarious joy that comes to a man through his children—*their* belief, *their* innocence, *their* spontaneous delight and ungrudging passion. He had foreseen all kinds of cataclysmic changes coming in the future—Joy leaving home, Joy marrying, Joy having children of her own one day. But he had not foreseen this closing of a door against him, this banishment from her world, this excommunication.

He would have turned cartwheels, stood on his head, quacked like a duck, told sixty-nine dreadful jokes, if he thought it would return the smile to his daughter's face. He remembered the fairy stories of kings offering half their kingdoms for one laugh from the princess. But he felt like a magician who has let his skills lapse. He could not remember, now it came to it, how to pull rabbits, or even where to start looking for the top hat to do it. 'Oh, Annie,' he said to his wife. 'She's so . . . *sad.*'

Anne Shepherd had had a nasty scare. Joy's sudden inexplicable disappearance on an unscheduled coach ride had thrown her mother into a panic, but of course she had played it down to her husband, pretended to know all about it, pretended she had given her permission. Lately such damage limitation was reflex. Anything to avoid his predictable outrage, the reflex bad temper he brought to every crisis these days. The coach ride had ended in death. What if it had been Joy who died? The fright and the relief combined to produce in her a fierce physical depression. She simply hadn't the energy nor the inclination, for once, to give her husband what he wanted, to tell him it was all fine, nothing to worry about. It was not.

So Jack Shepherd went unconsoled, and that too unnerved him. He had to *do* something. Now he came to think about it, he had always been surrounded by smiles; it was one of the reasons he had felt no need to smile himself: everybody in his family seemed happy enough without it. Now he looked about him in a fever of helplessness.

No one in the whole damn hotel was happy! Ivy Partridge was weeping in Colin Partridge's arms now. The Halliwells were rowing furiously about a broken toy, the L'Estrange children were retaliating for once—'But our mum says . . .'—and the British Legion were dividing into factions. The women, for the most part, wanted to be discreetly sympathetic, to cause the Partridges as little trouble in their bereavement as was possible, given the fact that they were marooned on the premises by the lack of a coach. The men, though, being largely of military background, were forming ranks, preparing to be angry, compiling a list of their grievances against Forever Xmas: no turkey, no Santa, no coach, no presents . . . Jack Shepherd opened the door of the cupboard under the stairs.

'Where are the presents for these people?' he asked Holly who was sitting in the meter cupboard among the stuffed stockings.

She looked up at him, her face awash with tears, her eyes so red and hostile that a lesser man might have backed out, apologizing. But Jack Shepherd held his ground, 'Where are the presents? And a pair of red trousers. He must have had a spare pair, your grandpa.'

Holly, when she saw what was in his mind, took him along to Felix Cox's room, beyond the kitchen. It was unremarkable enough accommodation, except (Jack noticed) the walls were entirely covered with thank-you letters and pictures from children, and with photographs sent after visits to Forever Xmas. There was F.C. with twins on his lap, F.C. with a chicken balanced on his head, F.C. reading stories to a group of toddlers, F.C. twirling an umbrella in a song-and-dance routine with six schoolgirls. The children all had the same look on their faces that Jack (now he thought back) had seen on Mel's. Rapture. Faith. Joy.

Some of the pictures were framed: Colin and Ivy holding hands with a very young Holly, no Christmas in sight. And a Lakeland view taken from somewhere high up, remarkable, after all the rest, for its total absence of people. Glancing at Holly, he saw a similar emptiness in her, space in her which lacked the presence of her marvellous grandfather.

The trousers were small for Jack, and the boots pinched as he walked back up the hall. But the jacket which he took without a word from over his daughter's clasped hands, was roomy enough. She looked at him with extreme suspicion, anticipating bad taste or disastrous misjudgement.

But Jack Shepherd, once he set his hand to a job, brought all his energies to bear. For a time, he had been expending all such energies on his work, but just at present work meant standing in for the absent F.C., helping the Partridges out in a crisis, giving the Legionnaires fewer grounds for complaint.

And when it came to it, he rather enjoyed the role. He flirted with silly pensioner ladies who laughed raucously in his ear, told jokes to ex-army men who called him a charlatan for being clean-shaven, but chortled as they said it. 'The Archbishop of Canterbury, the Head Rabbi, and the Chief Scout were all on an aeroplane plummeting to earth, but there were only two parachutes . . . ' He was good. He was very, very good.

Anne Shepherd watched in amazement. Her daughter came up beside her, and they exchanged disbelieving glances. 'Where's Mel? Find Mel. He's got to see this.'

But before Joy could go in search of her little brother, the french windows of the parlour opened and rain billowed into the room, as material as the streaming curtains. Behind the rain, his clothes so slick wet and clinging that he gleamed from head to foot like a seal, came Mr Angel, the Environmental Health officer. Leaves were stuck to him like fledgling feathers, and there were grazes on his hands and on the shins below his rucked up trouser-legs.

The roomful of people turned, as one, and stared at him with an intensity of interest which, for a moment, left him unable to speak. His mouth was cold, too, and not quite under his control. Joy slipped behind her mother, hiding.

'The little boy,' said Angel, pointing backwards through the french windows with a flipper-like flap of one arm. His supercilious voice was oddly uncertain. 'The little boy . . . ' he said again.

'Mel?' said Santa Claus, rising to his feet.

'I think he may have gone off up the mountain.'

10

Absent Friends

Over Cold Pike it took its stand, that concatonation of electricity, that belly of cloud gorged on eight weeks of sweltering heat. Claps of thunder vied to out-roar each other, erupting three, four, five times in as many seconds, and the strobe lightning made the mountain appear to move, to shift restlessly, to be stirring into life.

Jack Shepherd had to be restrained from going straight out into the rain, rigged up as Santa Claus. Ivy Partridge hung on his arm while her husband fetched out waterproof jackets and trousers, fell boots and torches. The coach arrived just then, driven back from Workington by a police officer, but the British Legionnaires showed no interest in going home. They offered to help in the search. Old ladies pulled shower bonnets from their handbags, covered their newly set hair and prepared, at a word, to sally out into rain that fell as if from a sluice. Meanwhile others were already searching the house from basement to loft, calling and calling with their flat northern vowels and sharp northern friendliness. Their husbands became militarily brisk, demanding maps, directions and, above all, information.

'What did he *say*? Where did he *say* he was going?' they asked Mr Angel over and over again. 'Why didn't you stop him?'

'I was stuck up the bloody tree!' Angel protested, not for the first time. 'The kid didn't seem to think . . . He didn't seem to mind that I . . . ' Wild-eyed, Angel shot nervous glances at the lost child's mother, not wanting to sound selfish and whinging, but at the same time wanting to exonerate himself. 'I sent him indoors—to fetch help—but he was just too . . . ' Surely the mother knew the random chaos of her child's thought processes, the boy's complete egocentricity, the irrational witterings children in general came out with?

'The Angel on the Christmas tree!' said one or two of the Legionnaires, aghast with understanding. 'We didn't believe him. The Angel on the tree!'

'He seemed intent on going up to "Santa's Special Place",' said Angel embarrassed by the sentimentality of the phrase. 'That's all he said, I swear.'

On either side of the fireplace Joy and Holly stood like book-ends. Circumstances had stepped between them that were too terrible to allow something as frivolous as friendship. 'He got this idea in his head,' Joy started to say. 'Mel thought Mr Angel was . . . Well, was a . . . '

'Mel thought Mr Angel really might be how he sounded,' said Holly briskly, struggling with the bases of her anorak's zip.

'How I sounded?' said Angel, his wet face and hair actually steaming in the heat of the room.

'You know . . . an angel,' muttered Joy.

'*He thought I was a real angel!?*'

' . . . so he wouldn't have thought it was particularly odd for you to be in a tree, would he?' said Holly. She was lacing up her fell boots now, resting each foot in turn on the arm of the sofa.

'But he *knew*—No! Don't give me that! He knew what I was!' protested Angel, dancing with outrage. The Legionnaires looked him over, looking for but not finding any resemblance to an angel. 'He said to me: "You're in charge of health! You're in charge of safety." You can't tell me . . . '

The elf for whom he had displayed such an arrant and personal dislike, looked at him coldly and said, 'Don't you think that's the sort of thing an angel might be put in charge of?'

Someone laughed and then, in embarrassment, turned the laugh into a cough: Mr Angel wondered if it was him. Everyone in the room was looking at him now. He saw accusation in their eyes—them holding him to blame for not being an angel. In point of fact, they were still looking to him for some further clue as to where Mel might have gone, but Angel could not bear their concentrated stare. He retreated back through the french doors—colliding with them because one had blown shut behind him—and ran for his car.

He fumbled blindly for several seconds with the boot lock, then pulled out walking boots and green Peter Storms and an emergency breakdown lamp.

'Leave this to us, sir,' said a police officer passing by wearing a yellow mac with bands of luminous white. (The officer who had brought back the coach had fetched in the officers from down by the gate.) But Mr Angel was impervious to advice. The little boy had mistaken him for an angel, and that, in the vacant reeling of Angel's rain-soaked head, burdened him with the responsibilities of an angel. The only way he could gain release from this new, fearful charge would be if he found the boy and brought him down off the mountain. Otherwise he would be trapped within the misunderstanding like a fly in amber. An angel in amber. Condemned to an everlasting fall from grace. Never had his name weighed so heavy on Mr Angel's shoulders: heavy as a pair of rain-sodden wings.

Holly finished lacing her boots and went out too through the french doors. Joy, startled into action, followed her, though without a coat or a plan or even a working grasp of the facts. All she recalled was her last unkindness to Mel, shouting and bullying him until his

82

face was as red as if she had slapped him. A huge foreboding overhung her, as violent and dark as the storm over Cold Pike. Unformed, unspoken, it nevertheless told her: if Father Christmas could die, then any degree of tragedy was possible today.

Anne Shepherd emerged, as from sleep, to a realization that both her husband and her son were on the mountain now, and that her daughter was bent on joining them. She looked down at the handkerchief in her hands and found it torn into ragged shreds which she threw in the grate before running out into the storm. 'Joy, come back! *Joy!*' The rain hit her in the face like a wet dishclout.

She caught up with her daughter where the donkey's meadow sloped suddenly upwards in a sharp incline. They were both wearing trainers. On the wet grass, the crêpe soles slipped as if on ice. First Joy fell on her face, and then her mother crashed down beside her. Third Wrinkle had been transformed into the Glass Mountain of fairy tale; unstudded shoes would no more carry them up the fellside than a monkey up a greased pole. Short of crawling on their hands and knees, they could do nothing but hug one another while the rain ran in rivulets down the hillside beneath them, and their hair swung round them like seaweed in a tide.

'I told him it was all his fault!' Joy wept. 'I told him the police would come and take us all away! Because of him!' She did not try to redeem herself. She did not want redemption. She was the sole and single cause of everything bad that had happened. When her mother began to shake her—shook her so violently that the rain spilled out of Joy's pockets—she thought it was anger fully deserved.

But her mother only shouted into her ear above the noise of the thunder, 'No, no, no. Forget that. He's gone looking for Santa's special place. You heard the man. That's what he said. It's *nothing to do with you*. He's gone looking for Santa's place. Do you understand? *It's not your fault!*

'It's true, F.C. did have a favourite spot.' Colin Partridge had to shout even to make his voice carry the short distance between himself and Jack Shepherd. 'Some place where he went bird watching. But it's been years . . . not since his angina started up . . . He couldn't have taken the boy there.'

'It's enough he talked about it. I expect Mel thought it was an ice grotto. Or a stable for the reindeer. Who knows what kids think?' Not me, that's sure, thought Jack Shepherd. What do I know about the workings of my own son's mind? Or my daughter's. Where had he been while Mel built himself castles in cloud-cuckoo-land, while Joy went sleigh-riding with a dying Santa Claus? It was as if he had been living underground and only emerged too late from hibernation to find his habitat destroyed, his cubs gone. That fatal slowness was still hampering him, too; his legs would not carry him as fast up the hill as he wanted them to.

'Damn Christmas! Damn Christmas! Oh, damn, damn the whole stupid . . . ' panted Colin Partridge, and it was not plain if he was sobbing with chagrin or with the exertion of the climb. 'If it weren't for our damn stupid Forever—'

'Stop!' said Holly. 'Stop it, Dad! What if F.C. could hear you? Don't.'

'It's your grandfather at the back of all this,' her father retaliated. But Jack Shepherd would not let that pass either.

'No. No. If I'd said earlier Mel could have Christmas, none of this would have happened.'

Angel could hear their raised voices, could see their torches flickering like a group of fireflies against the face of the hill.

But he did not join them. He held off at a distance—close enough to see what course they took up the fellside, but far enough not to become part of their quarrel. They were all blaming themselves . . . and yet Angel knew exactly where the blame lay. The little boy had asked him to help—had pleaded with him to help (though God knew with quite what), and the Angel in the Tree had spurned him. Angel knew that he, and no one else, was to blame if the child came to any harm.

He kept trying to calculate how far Mel might have got in the time it had taken to get down out of the tree, but time and distance had both become blurred by the torrential rain. He also kept trying to remember what the child had said to him at other times, his flat white face peering over the edge of the table, large ears red-rimmed with passion. So much more made sense, now that Angel saw devotion in that remembered face: devout angel-worship.

The sheep track Angel found himself on diverged from theirs, and he climbed more steeply, while they disappeared from sight around the curve of the hill. In his green waterproofs, he knew he was invisible, but still he did not turn on his lamp. He preferred to be invisible; it suited his frame of mind.

A movement and a noise made him shout with relief— 'Mel?' But it was only a sheep, kicking a stone with its sharp hoof, then standing motionless again in the mind-numbing downpour. Angel almost walked into it. Its yellow eyes dilated in a flash of lightning.

The police were higher up the mountain, searching, but no whistle sounded to signal success. An hour passed and no whistle sounded. The lights strung along the eaves were all that remained visible of the hotel far below; the lights and Charlie's coach in the car park. It was lit up from bumper to bumper with garish yellow light as if to lure Mel home like a moth.

Angel was cold. He had set off without gloves, and his hands were icy cold. He tried not to think how cold the boy must be by now, unprotected by waterproofs; how treacherous his footing must be in cloth, rubber-soled sneakers.

Had all this peril arisen from Angel's assault on the undercooked turkeys? Could it have done? He did not see how, and yet he sensed that it had. He would willingly have eaten every bone and sinew now of those carcasses, sooner than do it again. Angels do not savage turkeys, he thought. Angels have better things to do than seethe with petty spleen.

A wind, sucked over the contours of the Wrinkles by a collision of weather fronts, came howling past him. He must be near the brow of the hill. Lightning lit a standing shape, about the height of a boy. '*Mel!?*' It was a cairn.

Angel wondered what had become of the sky. Suddenly, where he expected clouds and the hollow navy of the storm, there was only dull, dense blackness. He had to wait for another lightning flash to see that a solid face of rock—Cold Pike—now reared up in front of him like a breaching whale. Rainwater poured off its plateau summit in a sparse curtaining waterfall. The top of the cliff actually overhung its base, the rockface being concave—like a wave in the act of breaking. Angel felt that at any moment the mountain could overwhelm him, swallow him up and leave no trace of his brief, microscopic life.

So much was he in awe of the looming cliff, and so blinded by rain that he all but stepped over the edge of one of the craters at its base. A jag of simultaneous lightning and thunder dazzled his eyes and left his ears singing. So he hardly trusted his senses when they suggested he had glimpsed a figure at the bottom of the crater, had heard a faint shout. Angel turned on his breakdown lamp and shone it into the pit. The debris of the ancient rockfall was strewn about like dinosaur bones in an excavation. The lightbeam, blunting itself against dark mud, suddenly puddled out over a pool of standing water. And there, knee deep in rainwater, his features pinched by cold like a knob of yellow Play-Doh, was Mel Shepherd.

Angel tested the strength of his voice, like a rope. 'Come on, Mel. Let's get you back down out of this wet.'

'Can't!' bleated Mel. 'I can't get out!' and then, swivelling round to show his mud-caked back, 'I fell.'

Mr Angel made reassuring noises. He was elated. Everything was going to be all right, after all. He had been expecting the worst, but now everything would be all right.

He was in such a hurry to reach the child—so intent on keeping Mel within the magical beam of his torch—that he failed to see the skid marks where Mel had lost his footing. The mud there was as black and slick as motor oil. Angel's own feet went from under him, his arms shot up, and his torch flew out of his wet hands.

He slid down the side of the grassy crater on the nylon of his waterproofs. Half-buried stones and boulders jarred into his flesh without slowing his slide. He landed, with a swampy gloop, in the pool of water, taking Mel's legs from under him so that the boy fell on top of him, cold face against cold face, cracking cheekbones.

The car lamp, meanwhile, tumbled away down the side of Third Wrinkle, exchanging its long white beam for an insistent flashing orange *blink blink blink*, like the lamp-room of a lighthouse smashed by the storm and falling, falling, falling into the black pandemonium of a moonless sea.

11

Keeping Christmas

The boy's teeth were chattering so loudly that Mr Angel could not judge in whose head the noise began. He got up as quickly as he could out of the pool of water (which was half a metre deep) but failed to keep the wetness out of his waterproofs. He could barely keep his footing. Several times he tried to climb back up the side of the bowl-shaped depression, towing Mel by the hand. But it was too smooth to get a handhold, and too steep to crawl up: he kept falling flat on his face against the mud, winding himself, steaming with the exertion. He could scarcely believe that the rain did not even pause to draw breath, continuing to beat down with the same tropical intensity.

Angel unzipped his jacket and held the little boy against the warmth of his chest. He had read articles about hypothermia.

'Are you going to fly us home?' The boy's words came hot through his wet shirt.

'I can't fly. I can't!' Angel responded with a kind of desperate exasperation.

'Why? Did you take your wings off?'

Angel tilted his head downwards to look at the face tight under his chin. It was still wide-eyed, brows arched, still credulous, still faithful to its own cherished delusions. 'Yes,' said the grown-up. 'Yes, I had to. They got sopping wet. They don't work when they're wet, you see.' There. It was easy. Lying.

'I couldn't find him,' Mel explained. 'F.C. I looked for his special place. All over. But I couldn't find it. Don't *you* know? Can't we go there? It'll be warm there!'

Mr Angel cleared his throat. 'I've never actually been there myself. I think it must be on top—above—up there,' and the local government official turned his face up towards the rain and the over-arching cliff-face. 'You can't get there on foot. You need the . . . the special Golden Ladder.' It got easier. Just like making excuses or exaggerating.

'But he's got my sister!' said Mel obstinately. 'He took my sister. Why didn't he take me?'

'Oh.' Angel was confused. The time spent locked in his room or stuck in the tree had robbed him of the facts. 'Ah well, maybe he plans to take you there tomorrow. Yes. That must be it. And he'd have to get her back by suppertime, wouldn't he? Or your mother would worry. So he must be back at the hotel. We'll soon see, won't we?'

Mel chewed his lip. 'But the police'll get him, there! Joy said!'

'What would the police want with Father Christmas?'

Mel pursed his trembling lips. 'I won't snitch,' he said.

Angel felt his grasp of the situation slipping away. 'Look. I won't let them take him. OK?'

'Cross your heart and hope to die?' Mel's faith in the Angel's powers of intervention were still intact.

'Cross my heart and hope to . . . ' Angel looked around him at the black, imprisoning banks. 'He'll be there. Trust me,' he said.

And that seemed to put an end to all Mel's misgivings. He wrapped his arms and legs tightly round Mr Angel and cuddled close against him, contented. Angel alone was left with the problem of keeping this small soaked boy alive in the bottom of a flooded pit for the duration of the night without any means of summoning help.

'What did God say?' asked Mel's muffled, weary voice. 'When you visited.'

'He was out,' said Angel flatly.

Holly saw it out of the corner of her eye—like a shooting star fallen to earth and bouncing, bounding down the mountainside: a Christmas orange rolling in and out of sight. When it came to rest, the orange glow continued to blink on and off, on and off, beckoning through the cascading rain. What if someone had thrown it, to summon help? she thought. Or what if someone had been holding it while it fell?

'I see something!' she called after her father. 'Over there. Something fell!'

They tracked sideways round the hill. The breakdown lamp kept blinking all the while—a sturdy piece of equipment as recommended by the RAC. The Royal Angel Corps, thought Holly.

'It's Mr Angel's lamp,' she said. 'I saw him get it out of his car.'

And so they all began to call: Holly and her father and Mr Shepherd, mentally cursing Angel for detracting from the search for Mel, scared at the prospect of yet another casualty. 'Mr Angel! Mr Angel!'

'Are you there?'

'Angel?!'

The thunder kept up like a sheet metal workshop, as though giants were panel-beating Cold Pike with lump hammers. And in between the thunderclaps was the soughing of the wind and the hiss of the rain: an undercurrent of ceaseless noise.

* * *

'Over here! Over here!' yelled Angel, but there was phlegm in his throat, and fright too. He could not make them hear. He got to his feet, balancing on the rock whose fall from the brink of Cold Pike had gouged out this treacherous pit at its base. '*Over here!*' All around, the rainwater was rising, filling up the pit. He had lifted Mel on to the rock and climbed up beside him, but the water too was climbing, filling the pit like a cistern. He no longer dared wade to the slope and try yet again to climb out. Besides, Mel was now cold to the touch—as cold as wet-fish on a slab. Even in Angel's waterproof jacket he engendered no heat of his own, as if some inner wick had blown out by the storm. Mel must not be allowed to sink into torpor; he must be kept awake. The trouble was, Angel was so tired himself . . .

'Tell me again about Christmas,' Mr Angel said.

'You're not very good at remembering,' said Mel sleepily. 'I told you loads of times.'

'Tell me again,' said Angel. 'Don't go to sleep. Tell me all about Father Christmas.'

'I don't snitch,' said Mel, and when the thunder broke, in a triple percussion over their heads, the child did not even flinch.

'Just tell me about Christmas, then. The First Christmas. Last Christmas. Open your eyes. Tell me all about Christmas.'

'Everyone knows,' said Mel, his speech slurred, as if by strong drink.

'I don't. I know nothing. Tell me. You're the expert. Tell me everything.'

It was someone else who, turned back by the impassable barrier of Cold Pike, found the flooded pits along its base—all but fell into one before his torchbeam, like a magic wand, opened it, yawning, at his feet. They could not see his face in the dark, could see nothing, blinded by that white blade of sharp light. It might almost have been the Golden Ladder of Angel's imagination, until the moment that flat, broad, matter-of-fact, unexcitable, voice called down to them—'All right?'—and a flash of lightning lit up Charlie's face and broad, unexcitable, unremarkable, wet, flat cap.

It was Charlie who fetched the police to the hole. After that, the sound of whistles, more piercing than screams, shrilled and warbled and, even though the shushing rain tried to silence them, carried as far as Holly and her father, still searching lower down.

The rainwater falling over the brim of Cold Pike was blowing in a smoke-white spray, across the top of Third Wrinkle, so that the torch-lit scene looked like grainy cine film, the movement of the figures stilted and over fast. There was not a rope among them, and they were moving round the brink trying to work out a safe means of reaching the people trapped in the pit.

Then Jack Shepherd came at a run, out of the darkness. He went over the side feet-first, and feet-first he slid down the mud bank, gouging out twin furrows in the bank, until his feet splashed into the water. The pit was half full, and the splash sent a bow wave slopping across the surface, which swamped the rocky debris in the middle. Mr Angel and Mel appeared to be floating on the water itself, unsupported.

'Stay there, man!' shouted Angel. 'Just stay there!'

He laid Mel across both shoulders—he looked reminiscent of those sentimental pictures of the Good Shepherd bearing home the Lost Sheep. The arms of the rainproof jacket dangled down far beyond the boy's hands; the hood had flopped down to hide his head. 'Stay there, and I'll come to you!' shouted Angel.

His body was so numbly cold that he could not feel the water round it, as he waded chest-deep across the depression.

When he reached Jack Shepherd, his head was just on a level with the man's feet. Leaning forwards against the mud-wall, he offered his shoulders as a firm rest for Jack's feet, so that Mel was able to climb up his father's body into the outstretched hands of . . .

'It's the police,' said Mel, looking up, perched like a drab green parrot on his father's shoulder.

Jack Shepherd could feel Angel sinking under the weight, being pushed down into the mud, losing his footing.

'Yes, son. Quickly. Reach up to them. Reach up.'

The elf's head poked between the yellow police macs. Mel hardly recognized her with her hair plastered so flat to her head. 'Come on, Mel. You can do it! Come on!' she urged. But still he did not put up his hands.

'It's all right,' said Mr Angel, his mouth only just clear of the water. 'You've done nothing wrong. There's nothing to be afraid of. Nothing, understand?'

Mel raised up his hands, and a policeman's grip closed round his wrists, as steely as a pair of handcuffs.

New boulders fell from the rim of Cold Pike that night on to the grass hill below. But by then the rescue party had descended, skidding on the wet grass, loosing wet scree from the streaming fellside, but finding their way down by the grey dawn light. They carried Mel in a yellow police mackintosh, a man holding each corner. Smoke was curling out of one of the chimneys of Forever Xmas Hotel, making a long grey anvil over the roof. An ambulance stood alongside Charlie's coach.

At the news the boy was found, the British Legionnaires, who had dozed and searched and waited up all night in the parlour and dining room, wriggled swollen feet into their shoes and hurried blearily outside under borrowed umbrellas, to cheer and congratulate and welcome home the search party. They let off party poppers and threw streamers. In place of laurels, they crowned the returning heroes with paper hats.

The animals, who had taken shelter from the storm in the barn, looked out of its door, also spectators of the Grand Return.

A warm, sherbet-lemon light spilled out of the windows and doors, and there was a fire lit in the dining room grate, fuelled here and there by twists and screws of pink paper. The heatwave over, the long Lakeland building looked more at ease, more at home in its natural lakeland elements of grey drizzle giving way to broken sunshine. The ambulance was sent away. All Mel needed was rest, they said.

'Eee, chuck, you're a wet item,' said a motherly Legionnaire to Mr Angel, rubbing his cold hands, divesting him of his ruined lovat sports jacket.

But those who knew him held off, kept clear, left a cautious space between themselves and the man who had dismembered Christmas with a carving knife.

Across the space Angel said, 'D'you know? We saw a twite on the way down. Always wanted to see a twite. And there it was, large as life. A twite!'

'That's nice, chuck,' said the lady doubtfully, and went on rubbing his hands. No one asked just what a twite might be.

Mel had slept much of the way down. Now he wriggled upright on the sofa, and his head emerged out of the police mac. 'Is he here? Is F.C. here?'

His mother was thrown off-stride. She had forgotten to think up a reply to this most disastrous question.

His sister, Joy, after a night of helpless worry and no sleep, was thrown back in among the events of the previous day. She had forgotten Mel did not know. 'No,' she said unguardedly. 'No.' (The old lady whispered something to Mr Angel. His face registered shock.)

'Where is he, then?' asked Mel, sensing something bad.

'Gone,' said Joy. What else could she say?

Her father brushed a finger in front of his lips: he who had held out so long and hard against Christmas. 'Nipped up to the North Pole, I expect,' he said. 'Isn't that right, Holly?'

'But he hates the North Pole!' protested Mel. 'Horrible, dangerous, cold place! He said!'

'Still, he has to go there, now and then. To check out the Toy Factory,' said Holly gamely, taking up her role once more, struggling into character.

'But we were going to have Christmas today! He must've forgot all about me!'

'No. No. He didn't!' Colin Partridge, who half-way up the mountain had damned Christmas to hell, rallied to its cause now. 'He didn't forget you. You'll see.'

'Yes he did! He went off in the coach with Joy, but he never took me! Where did you go, you two? Why couldn't you take me?'

Joy felt cornered. 'He . . . he just did.' But she could not do it. She hadn't the energy. F.C.'s death, the search, the fright, the waiting: they had emptied her of any comfortable lies. 'He just wanted to explain,' she began feebly. 'Why he had to go away. He didn't think you would understand.'

A policeman came into the room to retrieve his mac and say goodbye. Mrs Shepherd thanked him profusely. Then Joy saw Mr Angel reach out and touch the man on the shoulder, asking him to wait, wanting a word in private. She could guess what *that* was about. Mr Starr and Ronnie, and how she and F.C. had helped them get away. So really, what did it matter what Joy said to her little brother? Why should she not just say: 'He's dead. Father Christmas is dead.' It was only a matter of time before Mel knew it anyway: saw through the whole stupid deceit of Christmas. Why this ludicrous struggle to keep the pretence going for one selfish, grasping, snitching little boy? Still Mel looked at her, waiting for her to go on, wanting a better solace.

Suddenly Mr Angel said, in a stage whisper which filled the parlour, 'I expect, Mel, that he wanted her to help choose your present.'

The whole room stared at him.

Mel was appeased. The universe had swung into line again, its concentric planets circling round him, the single sun. 'He'll come, then? And bring it? I can have my wish?'

'He'll come,' said Angel. 'You may not see him, but he'll come. He always keeps his promises.'

Mel smiled, closed his eyes, and instantly went back to sleep. The room breathed a corporate sigh of relief. Christmas had been kept: preserved all night and into the light of day, Christmas had been kept alight like a flame, preserved in the dreams and imagination of a single young child. It was as if everyone there had preserved their own innocence.

All except Joy. 'What did you wish for, Mel?' she asked loudly, stridently, knowing her brother would not stir. His face reddening in the heat from the fire, he was so fast asleep that, even with his eyelids part-opened by the tilt of his head, he did not rouse. 'Brilliant. Thank you, *Mister* Angel. Now all we need is for F.C. to come back and tell us what Mel wished for.' Her voice choked on a glut of unshed tears. 'Except that he can't actually do that, can he?'

Mr Angel, his hair re-curling spontaneously as it dried and recovering its golden colour in the firelight, sat down on the sofa and ran his fingers through Mel's hair. 'I can,' he said. 'But first I must catch the police. I need a word with them before they go.' And he hurried out of the room, his movements rather stiff and painful.

12
Forever England

Joy and Holly exchanged glances. Joy nearly started after him. But there was nothing to be done. They waited, their breath between their teeth, two criminals who had aided and abetted an escaped felon. They could hear the murmur of voices in the hall: Mr Angel talking to the police.

But then the front door closed and the squad car outside drove off, and Mr Angel came back, jingling his car keys, and said he would go out and buy the present, if that was all right with Mr and Mrs Shepherd.

At first they thought it could never be done in time. Then, when it was done, when everything was ready for the surprise, they thought Mel would never wake up. He slept on and on, impervious to the noisy departure of the Legionnaires' coach, undisturbed by the bad-tempered banging of car doors as the Halliwells checked out. The L'Estranges left, too, their Christmas over for another four months. Everyone remaining moved about in that odd frame of mind brought on by lack of sleep, anticlimax, and regret.

Mr Angel phoned in sick to the Environmental Health Department, then prepared a Spanish omelette with eggs he found himself in the barn. 'It's domestic consumption if I cook it myself,' he told Mr and Mrs Partridge who perched on the edge of the kitchen table feeling awkward and hiding the home-made mayonnaise from sight. Ivy was wearing a smart black suit and her hair in a black, net snood. She was in mourning for her father, though, to the strains of Glen Miller, looked more like Mrs Miniver braving the Blitz.

When Jack Shepherd hung up the striped stocking at the foot of Mel's bed, he wore the red Santa jacket, just in case he was spotted, but Mel was still out like a light.

Joy and Holly passed the time making a parcel for pass-the-parcel, layer after layer of the L'Estranges' discarded wrapping paper around a wallet of felt-tip pens, and between each layer a gold chocolate coin.

'Of course, *you* shouldn't really know what's at the middle,' said the elf.

'Why not?'

'Because you're a guest. You'll be doing the passing. You're a child.'

'No more than you!' retorted Joy hotly.

'Oh, I know,' said Holly. 'But that's half my trouble. *I* shouldn't know what's in the middle either. It doesn't do to know exactly how Christmas is put together. That's when it starts to fall apart.'

'So how can you go on doing all this?' Joy waved a hand, contemptuous of the hotel and all it represented, trying out her new-found cynicism.

'I don't know,' said Holly meekly. 'F.C. made it, and F.C.'s gone now, isn't he? He was the middle of everyone's parcel. He was the surprise prize. Mad as a cat in a tumble-drier, so you never knew what he was going to do next. You think that was put on for the guests? It wasn't. He made it Christmas for us, too. This place would have gone west years ago if it hadn't been for him.'

Joy could almost feel the rattling of the coach underneath her once again, the heat of the sand, the cold of the ice-lolly. It was like a memory from times much longer ago; like being Mel's age. 'I wish . . . ' she began, but saw the word trigger in Holly that obligation to listen to other people's wishes. 'It's all right, You can't grant this one. I was just going to say, I wish there was a mountain we could go up and fetch *him* back.'

'Oh. Yes. Thank you. So do I,' said Holly. 'So do I.' And they sat sadly after that, the tips of their shoes touching, and the parcel between them unfinished on the floor.

Mel woke with that momentary pang of anxiety which comes with being somewhere that is not home: also the feeling that something bad has happened which no amount of effort can undo. His sleepy brain was slow to make sense of the twists of colour mooring all four walls of the room to the lampshade in the middle. A pink paper Santa, stuck up with double-sided tape, had come adrift from the wall and leaned outwards at a reckless angle, like a diver on the topmost diving board. For some reason Mel pictured the sea, and seagulls crying. The window glass was weeping with raindrops, too. Though the bedroom was empty, he had the impression he was being watched.

Various grazes on his knees and hands were faintly sore. Gingerly, he eased himself up into a sitting position. There, at the end of his bed, Christmas was laid out to greet him. There was a bulging striped woollen stocking, a sticker book, and a big blue-and-red beachball.

'He came?' said Mel aloud, but the person he had sensed was outside did not answer or put their face round the door. Instead, feet thumped down the stairs.

'He's awake!' called a distant voice.

Mel crawled down the bed to grab his stocking, but saw, over the footboard, a small wicker linen-basket, moving of its own accord. Mel looked at the door out of the corner of his eye, and retreated with his stocking to the middle of the bed. Head down, he pulled out hollow chocolate animals, a pencil with a springy monster on the end, a metal puzzle, an orange, a matchbox car, a giant dice.

They told you never to look at the sun, never to touch fire. Mel was not stupid; he knew how to avoid pain. He would not look, he would not touch. That way, he could not be disappointed. He even withdrew a little up the bed, away from the creaking linen-basket.

People were converging on him from all corners of the hotel. Into the room they came, wishing him a Happy Christmas: his sister, the elf, Mr and Mrs Partridge, Mr Angel, his mum and dad. They all had a pent-up look, as if they were holding their breaths. He recognized the look, but he was not going to ease their predicament. He *would not* look in the basket.

Suddenly, from the foot of the bed came a high, whistling whimper. Mel jumped down, spilling sweets and toys out of his lap. 'He did! He did! He did! He did! He did!' he said under his breath. All his loose teeth moved in their sockets as he ground them hard together to stop his heart escaping out of his mouth.

He threw open the lid of the basket. Inside was a collie puppy, black and orange, with a bib of white fluff. It scrabbled up at him, nose like a doorstop, liquid black eyes, ears like the flaps of envelopes. It jumped on its two back feet, trying to get out: the paws over the basket's edge were white as snow.

'Well?' said his mother. But Mel felt no need to speak to any of them. He was no longer dependent on them for happiness. He had been given his own inexhaustible treasure chest of happiness. . . . Besides, if he looked at his father, the spell might break: he might say no to the dog. *He* would never have brought Mel a dog. F.C. was the only person in the world who would have done that.

'He came, Dad,' said Mel at last.

'Looks like it,' said his father.

'Look what he brought me, Dad.'

'A dog, eh,' said his father gruffly. 'Dogs are a big responsibility.'

'I told you he didn't go to the North Pole.' Mel spoke quickly, urgently, to stop his father spoiling things, to stop him forbidding the miracle. 'You can't keep dogs at the North Pole. Only huskies and reindeers.'

'Dogs need a lot of . . .'

'F.C. brought him, so I have to keep him, you see? He knew, Dad! He knew I had to have a dog! I never told him a dog. Any animal I said. But he knew!'

'You'd best call him Santa, then,' said his father.

'Or Felix,' said his sister. Mel liked 'Felix', though he did not understand.

In that moment, the world was made perfect again. Man had never fallen from grace. God had never felt any disappointment in His Creation. For Mel, Paradise was both present and thriving. As he held the dog to his face and rubbed his cheek against the silky fur, his belief in miracles was absolute. His world had been redeemed by Christmas.

So F.C. had, to all intents and purposes, visited while Mel slept. Though it had been Mr Angel who drove like a demon round the Cumbrian countryside to effect the purchase, though the linen-basket belonged to Mrs Partridge and the cash had come out of Jack Shepherd's back pocket, still F.C. got the credit. And because of that, it was impossible to entertain the idea of his death. If Felix Cox had died, he was alive again now, in Mel's convictions, and that made him alive too for Ivy Partridge and Holly. It had to be Christmas Day that day: nowhere else was big enough to house the celebration.

* * *

Holly put her hand through Mr Angel's arm as they went down the stairs. 'Do you like birds, Mr Angel?'

'Why? Is it turkey again for lunch?'

'No, I mean the live kind. You're wearing an RSPB tie. You have a Slimbridge sticker on your car. I thought—'

'Yes, I do do some birdwatching,' said Angel cautiously, extricating his arm. He was not accustomed to being touched.

'Only I'll take you up to Bird Top today if you like. It's Grandad's favourite . . . Grandad used to like going there, before his heart got bad. He took me. There's ravens and twite—and buzzards sometimes.' It amused her to see such childlike delight on a grown man's face. 'Just as well Mel told you about his wish. Joy and I, we wondered what Mel was finding to talk to you about. Now we know. His wish.'

'We talked about a lot of things up Cold Pike,' said Angel unnervingly. 'It was a long night.'

'Joy and I, we wondered . . . ' Holly started once, started again, but could find no gentle road through the minefield.

Joy, on the other hand, came thudding down the stairs behind them and said it straight out: 'What did you want with the police?' She was unconvincingly breezy. Holly went as rigid as a greyhound.

Angel looked at them through narrowed eyes. 'To find the nearest dog breeders, of course. It's not so easy just to find a puppy these days. Not since pet shops stopped selling pets. But the police knew someone straight off. Always a reliable source of information, I find, the police.'

Joy and Holly breathed an audible sigh of relief and their hunched shoulders dropped. There would be no wail of sirens now, no handcuffs and cautions, no interrogations. Mel had not snitched to Mr Angel about the Starrs.

The squad car was indeed gone from beside the gate, the search for the escaped prisoner had moved on to pursue some other line of guesswork. Within the day, Starr would be back at the prison gates, turning himself in. The girls' brief careers as criminals had come to a discreet close.

The music playing downstairs was Glen Miller's band, because that was Ivy's favourite. People ate desultorily at the kitchen table—microwaved pizza and pastries. Their body-clocks were all wrong after the long night, and anyway the puppy was too much of a distraction to allow for a proper set meal.

They pulled no crackers. (Mel said it would frighten the dog.) No one wore paper hats. No one watched the Queen's Speech. The puppy got hold of Mel's new beachball and punctured it, even with milk teeth. No one played Trivial Pursuit or Monopoly, or fell asleep in front of the TV. The elf wore jeans and trainers. No one scribbled a list of presents received, tormented by the prospect of all the thank-you letters. No one looked back nostalgically at the year just gone; there was a kind of tacit understanding that the least said about it the better. Half the guests went birdwatching on Bird Top where they fed their Christmas cake to the twites.

But it was the Christmas Mel would always remember— would recall fifty years later—would remember, along with the smell of privet hedges and Vick Rub and old trainers, as the essence of childhood. It was, as the storybooks always say, the best Christmas anyone could remember.

'So. In your reports. Do we pass muster, Mr Environmental Health?' Holly asked pertly, as Angel watched delightedly the ravens circling like omens of wickedness over his head.

'You pick a shrewd time to ask,' said Angel without lowering his binoculars.

Holly shrugged. 'I was just interested. I'm a professional.'

Angel snorted with laughter. 'No, you're not. You're an eleven-year-old kid. And no, since you ask. No, you don't pass muster. You serve undercooked turkey, and that's a menace to public health.'

'We never do!'

'Undercooked turkey could kill someone. I could close you down for that, if I had a mind to.'

To his astonishment Holly said, with a haughty toss of her head, 'You needn't bother. Dad's going to wind up the business anyway.'

'Oh!' Angel was wrong-footed. He who had wrung blood from a turkey by sheer willpower, whose wish had been to see Forever Xmas expunged from the world map, found he did not like having his wish granted, particularly by its resident elf. 'But why?' he said.

'It's no good without F.C.,' she said. 'And this scare with Mel . . . it's easier catering for grown-ups. The insurance is cheaper if you keep out the under-fives.'

In the face of such icy business acumen, Angel quailed. Just when he had found out a thing or two about Christmas, he did not think he liked having it cancelled forever and a day. As she went to move away, wander off, leave him to his birdwatching, he commented knowingly, 'Give my regards to the Starrs then, won't you?' She flinched and jumped round. Keeping the binoculars pointing at the sky, he added, 'You must get a pretty good view of them hereabouts.'

Jack Shepherd and Joy did not go up to Bird Top. Ivy Partridge gave them a lift down to the garage to collect their car. Its radiator was mended.

'I was thinking we might give Linstock a miss,' he said, as he re-adjusted the driver's seat. 'Ring up. Say we can't make it after all.'

'Go straight home, you mean? Mel would like that. He

could get the dog a bit house-trained before he goes to school.'

'Well, actually, I thought the Partridges could look after the puppy for a couple of days while we go over—'

'That would be perfectly satisfactory,' Ivy chimed in, brushing dog hairs off her black suit.

'Leave the puppy?' said Joy. 'Mel'd never leave the puppy.'

'He might have to. Just for a while. That's his Christmas present. And you haven't had yours yet.'

'Mine?'

'Yes. I thought we could go over to Blackpool. You know. Stay at the Imperial, do the donkeys and the Tower and Sea World. All that. You like the seaside best, don't you? That was always your favourite. Sea and sand. You could go with just your mother, if you like—if you don't want Mel muscling in on your Christmas. I could stay on with him here. But I'd rather be a part of it if—'

'No,' said Joy.

'No?' He recoiled and stood with the mechanic's plastic sheeting crumpled against his chest.

'I mean, no. You come too. I'd prefer it with you there. We can pick up the puppy on the way home, yes.'

Those few days, free of guests, were all it took for the Partridges to replan their future. Despite the funeral (perhaps because of it), they managed to take down the lights from along the front of the house, to strip the bedrooms of their decorations, to empty the ready-made stockings, to cancel future bookings. By the time the Shepherds called in to collect Felix the puppy, the house had already taken the strangest step back through Time. There were tin hats hanging from hooks in the barn, and Dig for Victory posters pasted to its corrugated wall. There was a Union Jack flying in the car park, and a smell of Spam frying.

'I don't know why we never thought of it before!' Colin Partridge greeted them. 'It's always been a passion with us. Well, F.C. never thought much to it, but then he was *there*, like, and got bombed. Ivy and I we love it. The films. The music. The clothes. We thought: concentrate on the old folks. It was F.C. who was so good with the kiddies. We're better with the old folks. Lots of nostalgia, we thought. Got to look ahead: nostalgia sells these days. Ivy's trying out some recipes now. She does a wonderful carrot cake, I can vouch for that. No dried eggs, though. That'd be a waste, given the chickens. We've got all the music and, you know, I video everything about Churchill. Hero of mine, always was.' The ideas spilled out of him like bombs over Dresden. 'Not that we want to glorify the fighting or owt, but the old folk, they're so appreciative of everything—Well, you saw what great characters we get off the coaches . . . We always wished we could just cater for the old folks . . . Forever England. That's what we thought we'd call it. Holly thought of it. Forever England.'

'What's Holly's part in all this?' asked Joy's mother, imagining: a land girl, or possibly a skinny Marlene Dietrich, in place of the elf.

'Oh, she'll be too busy with schooling,' said Colin. 'Best leave her out of our fandanglings—at least during the studying years. Best to plan round her these days. Only fair, wouldn't you say?' Anne Shepherd said yes, she thought that was probably for the best.

Even so, when Joy tracked her down, Holly was standing in front of F.C.'s bedroom mirror trying on a variety of hats—a man's trilby, an RAF cap, a tin hat. She stopped at a GI's jaunty forage cap which suited her. 'They had all this stuff in the attic. They collect it. Once we decided, it all just seemed to spill out; as if it had been waiting to take over.'

'Aren't you sorry? To see Christmas go?'

'No! This is great. This is about them. They're not trying to please someone else: they're doing it because it pleases them.'

'So did Christmas once. You said.'

'And now it will again! You will come, won't you? When we're set up? You will come and stay?'

In the face of Holly's excitement, Joy felt like the cynic now. She could see that Holly would involve herself just as much as before, studies or no studies. She was not the one being exploited—she was a willing partner in her parents' dreams. Joy almost wished she could reach out a hand and restrain her. 'There can't be many people left who remember the Forties,' she pointed out as diplomatically as she could. 'I mean, the ones who do . . . aren't they all terribly old?'

But Holly did not see what she meant. 'Oh, that's all right! We'll put in a lift!' she said triumphantly.

So Joy had to wait till they were on the road again, and catch her father's eye in the driving mirror before she could voice her chief worry:

'Quite soon, there won't be anyone left who remembers the War, will there, Dad?' she said, above the noise of her brother laughing, the puppy scrabbling against the tailgate. 'So this "Forever England" of theirs: it can't last very long, can it?'

Her mother turned round and handed her one of the sandwiches Ivy Partridge had given them for the journey. Egg mayonnaise. No turkey left. 'No, it can't last for ever. But then nothing ought to, chicken. Don't you think? Very probably nothing should.'

Geraldine McCaughrean is one of the most highly-acclaimed living children's writers. She has won the Carnegie Medal, the Whitbread Children's Book Award (three times), the Guardian Children's Fiction Award, and the Blue Peter Book of the Year Award, and is known and admired for the variety and originality of her books, as well as her stunning storytelling skills.

Among her other books for OUP are *The Kite Rider, The White Darkness, Stop the Train, and Not the End of the World*. In 2005 she was chosen by the Trustees of Great Ormond Street Hospital for Children to write the official sequel to *Peter Pan*. The result was *Peter Pan in Scarlet* which was published worldwide to huge critical acclaim in 2006 and became an instant classic.

Neverland is calling again...

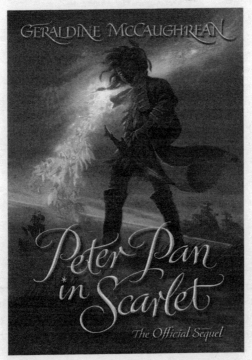

GERALDINE McCAUGHREAN

Peter Pan in Scarlet

The Official Sequel

The first ever official sequel to J.M. Barrie's *Peter Pan*

Something is wrong in Neverland. Dreams are leaking out—
strangely real dreams, of pirates and mermaids, of warpaint and
crocodiles. For Wendy and the Lost Boys it is a clear signal—
Peter Pan needs their help, and so it is time to do the
unthinkable and fly to Neverland again.

But back in Neverland, everything has changed—
and the dangers they find there are far
beyond their dreams ...

Great Ormond Street Hospital Charity

OXFORD

Geraldine McCaughrean
Winner of the Whitbread Children's Book Award

The White Darkness
'Astonishing' *Guardian*

ISBN 978-0-19-272618-6

Captain Oates, hero of the Antarctic, has been dead for nearly a century. But not in Sym's head. In there, he is her constant companion, her soul mate, her adviser. It is as if he walked out of the Polar blizzard and into her mind. In fact, if it were not for him, life might be as bleak as the Antarctic Wilderness.

When a short family expedition spirals out of control, Sym is forced to ask herself a question that becomes a matter of life or death: is it madness to stake one's happiness on someone who isn't there?

'A breathtakingly fine novel'
Bookseller

'McCaughrean's imagination is fierce, tireless, unpredictable'
Observer

'Astonishing'
Guardian

ISBN 978-0-19-275432-5

Everyone knows the story of the Ark. The flood rising, the animals entering two by two. Noah. But what about the women and children? Did they all accept Noah's orders to ignore their friends and neighbours struggling in the water?

When Timna does the unthinkable—when she defies her father and saves a life—she knows her fearful secret may bring death and disaster on board. If it does, one thing is certain. There will be nowhere to run.

'A tour de force by a brilliant writer'
Guardian

'Finely written, hugely challenging and rewarding'
Jan Mark, *TES*

ISBN 978-0-19-271881-5

For Cissy and her family, a new life is beginning on the prairies of Oklahoma. It's 1893 and for them and their fellow settlers, a bright future seems set to arrive along the Red Rock Railroad track. But when they refuse to sell their homes to the greedy railroad company, its boss swears his trains will never stop there again. How can the little town of Florence hope to survive without the railway? Its inhabitants might as well pack up and go back where they came from.

But Cissy and her neighbours vow to *make* the train stop—to do whatever it takes, to risk whatever they must, no matter what consequences come hurtling around the bend . . .

'for a really good read, look no further than this excellent, unpredictable and engrossing novel from a genuine master of the imagination.'
Independent

'This funny, sad and insightful novel . . . has all the hallmarks of a modern classic.'
Guardian

'. . . a tense, fast-moving adventure story, sustained to the very last page'
Financial Times

ISBN 978-0-19-275528-5

Haoyou knows that his father's spirit is living high above him in the sky over Ancient China. He also knows that now it is his turn to follow his father—so, strapped to a kite, Haoyou is sent to fly among the clouds and the spirits of the dead.

This amazing story is unlike anything else you have ever read. Packed with action, adventure and a real taste of life in Ancient China, *The Kite Rider* was the winner of the Blue Peter 'Best Book to Keep Forever' Award and the Smarties Prize Bronze Award, and was shortlisted for the Carnegie Medal.

'a marvellous soaring story that gives you a glimpse into another world'
Guardian

'A masterpiece of storytelling'
The Times

'an author incapable of writing a dull sentence'
Nicholas Tucker, *Independent*

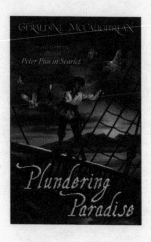

ISBN 978-0-19-271994-2

Nathan has always loved pirates. Their swashbuckling
adventures light up his dull life and give him something to
dream about. So when Tamo White, the son of a real life pirate,
suggests that Nathan and his sister go home with him to
Madagascar, it's too good a chance to miss. But can
Nathan and mousy Maud really survive on an island of
savages and cut throats?

'This must be the finest adventure story for years . . . A brilliant read.'
Guardian

'a superb adventure story—the literary equivalent of a good all
action movie.'
Good Housekeeping

'This swashbuckling adventure is not to be missed!'
Daily Telegraph

ISBN 978-0-19-275529-2

Inez and Maro can't believe their eyes when a hole appears outside their father's shop. Before long, there are holes all over town, undermining the buildings, undermining everyday life. There are strangers, too – desperados and entertainers, gunslingers and money-men. Rumours are rife: of monsters, murder and dreams come true.

It's started . . . the secret's out. People are coming from all over the country with a glint in their eye and hope in their hearts. And the word on everyone's lips is GOLD.

The action is non-stop in this thrilling adventure which won the Whitbread Children's Book Award.

'This novel is pure gold dust' *Times Educational Supplement*

'a rich tale of the lust for money that undermines an entire Brazilian town' *Guardian*

'This novel is a feat of imagination and genuinely awe-inspiring' *Books for Your Children*

ISBN 978-0-19-275203-1

Ailsa doesn't trust MCC Berkshire, the mysterious man helping out in her mother's antique shop. He tells wonderful stories about all the antiques, and his stories dazzle the customers, but everything he says is a pack of lies, isn't it?

Thick and fast the stories come: tales of adventure, revenge, mystery, and horror. But what is MCC's own story? Where is he from? And what will happen if his lies ever come face-to-face with the truth?

'a treat, written in a quirky, highly individual style which whirls the reader along until the surprise ending'
Guardian

'clever and entertaining'
Independent

ISBN 978-0-19-275290-1

Gabriel has no idea what the future will hold when he
runs away from his apprenticeship with the bad-tempered
stonemason. But God himself, in the shape of playmaster
Garvey, has plans for him. He wants Gabriel for his angel . . .

But will Gabriel's new life with the travelling players be any
more secure? In a world of illusion, people are not always what
they seem. Least of all Gabriel.

'This unforgettable book, which knows no age barrier,
should become a classic'
Evening Standard

'This is a very good novel, rich in uncluttered historical detail, written with
sensitive fluency, and with a gallery of memorable characters.'
Junior Bookshelf

ISBN 978-0-19-275091-4

Phelim is the chosen one, the only one, they say, who can
save the world from the dreadful monsters, the Hatchlings
of the Stoor Worm. But Phelim is only a boy—what can
he do? And where will he find the others who are supposed
to help him—the Maiden, the Fool, and the Horse? As Phelim
sets out on his quest, the words ring in his ears: 'You must
stop the Worm waking.'

'McCaughrean is a superb storyteller, and her tale is irresistible.
The real pleasure of this book is the powerful evocative prose—there
are memorable descriptions on every page.'
Times Educational Supplement

'From page one, you are in the hands of a superb storyteller. The writing
is so marvellous that you can open the book at random and find a brilliant,
memorable description. It's a horror story, an elemental
struggle, a search for identity. I wish I'd written it.'
Books for Keeps